EIGHTEEN

JENNY JAECKEL

Black Rose Writing | Texas

First printing

This is a work of fiction. Names, characters, businesses,
places, events, and incidents are either the products of the
author's imagination or used in a fictitious manner. Any
resemblance to actual persons, living or dead, or actual
events is purely coincidental.

ISBN: 978-1-68433-861-0
PUBLISHED BY BLACK ROSE WRITING
www.blackrosewriting.com

Printed in the United States of America
Suggested Retail Price (SRP) $19.95

Eighteen is printed in Sabon

*As a planet-friendly publisher, Black Rose Writing does its best to
eliminate unnecessary waste to reduce paper usage and energy
costs, while never compromising the reading experience. As a result,
the final word count vs. page count may not meet common
expectations.

Author Photo: Erika Lunder
Cover Art: Jenny Jaeckel
Editor: Neesa Sonoquie

For R & C

I'll be your mirror
Reflect what you are, in case you don't know
I'll be the wind, the rain and the sunset
The light on your door to show that you're home

—The Velvet Underground

PART ONE

The thing I wanted to tell you about, the thing I forgot to tell you about, was that time two years ago I saw seven rainbows all in one day, and I thought it was a good sign, but of what exactly I didn't know. It was before I started college, before I met Renee, and before I met George and messed things up with George, and my days started feeling like I was climbing over mountains made of a thousand sharp peaks.

But what you have to understand is that the day of the rainbows wasn't even a happy one. It was a single weather system of rainclouds and gaps of sun, and it stretched out over miles and miles of highway. I was on my way to Olympia, Washington, on this big old lumbering bus called the Green Tortoise, like a Greyhound but for hippies, with no seats just a big flat mattress and everyone's luggage stowed away underneath. We'd started out in San Francisco the night before. My friend Amy took me to the pick-up spot, and when they loaded in my huge black duffel bag with everything I owned inside, a woman behind me said, "Looks like someone's leaving home," and I almost started crying, though I wasn't even sure why.

I guess the idea of home was always one that slipped through my fingers. I don't mean that I never had a home. Some kids really don't have homes, and I never had to deal with anything like that. It's just that my parents were busy trying out all kinds of communes in different states and cities, or way out dirt roads with a lot of other people coming and going, and I was just along for the ride. And then when the two of them went their separate ways, things for me got even more scattered. By the time I got on the Green Tortoise, I'd lived in thirteen different places, and with a million different people, and a handful of those were people I'd gotten close to and then never saw again. Now I was going to an entirely new place, for college, and because I'd been out of school for a year I was excited to go, but I was also pretty terrified. Amy gave me this great big hug, and I would have told her that she was my best friend but we didn't really talk like that.

That night I slept, listening to the sound of the bus engine. It was the beginning of September, and when I woke up we were in Oregon, and rain was splashing against the windows. And all day, as we passed rivers and farms and cities and towns with names like Lebanon and Beaverton, and ugly as shit gas stations, and wound through evergreen-covered mountains, the sun kept breaking through the rain, and I watched the sky and saw all those rainbows. I was feeling so unsure, like I was an empty jar, rattling around inside this capsule of strangers, headed for a place I'd never laid eyes on, so, like I said, I took it as a good sign.

* * *

By the time we got to Olympia it was already getting dark. My dad had given me money for a taxi, to get from the bus to campus, and he'd helped me arrange for someone from the residential office to let me into the apartment after hours. The official move-in wasn't until the next day so I was the first one there, and I looked at all the empty rooms, wondering what my new life would be like and who would be in it and how I would be, walking around when it was all colored in.

I had my Walkman and most of my tapes, which saved me from the awful silence, and I ate trail mix for dinner, staring at the bare walls and thinking, *This is my new life.* After that I got into my sleeping bag, used my coat for a pillow and wrote a letter to my friend Hari, who was in school at UCLA. Then I read a section of *The Grapes of Wrath* with a flashlight. Amy had given it to me, saying that I couldn't live without reading it and that I had to make it through the first hundred pages to understand. By the time I started getting sleepy, Tom Joad had gotten out of prison and made it home, and when the grandma saw him she said, "Pu-raise Gawd fur vittory!" And I fell asleep repeating that line in my mind. *Pu-raise Gawd fur vittory... Pu-raise Gawd fur vittory...*

* * *

Every morning the whole first week I woke up feeling like there was a hive of bees in my stomach. I'd lie there trying to visualize them flying out through my belly button so I could halfway relax, but they hung around anyway, even though everything was fine. All my roommates seemed pretty nice. Renee, the one who had a room next to mine asked me if I wanted to share a phone line. I said I did and then I didn't see her for a few days because classes weren't starting right away and she left to go see her boyfriend who was going to Reed down in Portland.

By then I'd gotten my room more set up. The walls weren't bare anymore because I'd put up my hundreds of postcards. I'd collected most of them in the past year. Several I'd bought in San Francisco, like the black and white one of Frida Kahlo when she was young, and others I'd gotten from my high school friends. We'd all gone different places after graduation and we all wrote to each other. A lot of the postcards we made ourselves, because art was something we had in common, especially me and Amy. One of my favorites was one from Hari that he'd made out of a photo of him and some of his friends, posing like statues in front of a fountain.

I couldn't call anyone until the phone line got installed, and having all those cards around made me feel better. Gradually my internal bees settled down and I was getting organized. I wanted to find a way to deal with the compost, for one thing, since putting food scraps in the garbage was against my religion. One of my roommates said I should take it out to the college farm, which you got to on a path through the forest, and she said I could borrow her bike if I wanted and so I went, the first Saturday when the bucket was full.

***

The Washington forest was strange to me. I was used to oak trees and lacey light and space, and this was the opposite—deep and dark, stuffed with ferns and big cedars with heavy branches hanging down like old ladies in raincoats, and the sky on top like an iron lid. But I liked the maples that grew here and there, for their big yellow leaves that spun down on the wind and got caught up in the spokes of the bike, and I liked the smell of fall, like a cork from a wine bottle.

I was relieved when I got to the farm, because there was open space around me again, and a lot of grass. I understood grass. An old guy with a scraggly white ponytail and faded overalls was digging up one of the beds and he told me where to dump the bucket, and then he asked me to help him get a few escaped chickens back into the coop, these three hens that were casually pecking around. There was a swath of chicken wire held open by a weathered two-by-four, and I ran at the chickens with my arms out and they went squawking into the coop. I thought I had done a good job but the old guy goes, "You don't have to scare the shit out of them." I might have said, "You're right," or, "Sorry," but he'd already stalked off, and I stood there next to the bike and the empty bucket like a stupid human, feeling bad for the chickens, who were just minding their own business.

I actually kind of liked chickens. Watching them reminded me of commune life when I was a kid. Two of the places I lived with my mom had chickens and one of my chores was feeding them, and I thought how they walked was pretty hilarious, jerking their heads every time they took a step. Me and the other kids used to have chicken-imitating contests and make each other die of laughter, and it was a nice break from fighting over Cheerios or whose turn it was in the hammock.

* * *

By October I was getting acclimated to life at school. I got along with my roommates, classes were well underway and super interesting, and I loved my new job at Media Loan. I'd looked at the hundreds of job postings on a wall outside the admissions office and applied to a lot of them, but the one I really wanted was at Media Loan, because I'd been there on an orientation tour and was kind of fascinated. Back in Ukiah it was a big deal the day the library got a new photocopier. Amy and I had used up a handful of dimes making pictures of our hands and faces, and the shelves of Media Loan with their stacks of monitors and microphones and cameras, and audio recording stuff and amps and speakers, and racks of cables and bins of adaptors had a lot more art potential than that.

At the interview, the boss, Millie, asked me if I was responsible and everything, and then she asked me to tell her a joke. I wasn't prepared for that and I said the only one I could think of, about how Stevie Wonder burned his face by answering the iron, and I left all depressed because I thought I'd blown it. But she hired me, and I started training with the rest of the new staff and I was eager to learn, because I already had a such crush on the gear.

This one day during my shift I drew a cartoon of three BNC cables standing together dressed like rappers, with a heading that said "RUN-BNC" and I tacked it to the wall by one of the check-out desks. One of my co-workers, this guy named Calvin, stared at it and he goes, "This would make excellent t-shirts. I make t-shirts, I should make staff t-shirts." And just as I was about to say, "Sure!" the phone rang and he answered it by going, "Leave me alone?" instead of "Media Loan?" Then when he hung up and saw I was watching him he said, "Try it, nobody notices."

***

Later that afternoon Calvin and I were assembling a long list of equipment reservations, and got to talking, and we discovered we had both grown up in small towns. He said that as soon as he could he escaped to Seattle to be gay.

I said, "How did it go, being gay in Seattle?"

He smiled, "It went great." Then the phone rang, and Calvin answered, "Leave me alone?" But Millie, caught him, and she pointed her finger at him like she was throwing out a lightning bolt, and Calvin shrank down to nothing. Millie was a cool boss, but you didn't want to do anything to make her angry. She was very scary when she got angry, even though it was always reasonable, like the time a student returned a VCR with a dog's muddy footprint on it, or when this one girl pushed in a cartful of gear with all the cables dragging on the ground. Those people walked away pretty much burned down to their skeletons.

* * *

Lately I'd been checking out more equipment myself, ever since one of my professors showed us this very moody short film where all these wild horses were battling in slow motion, and then running through water and fire, and then plunging into deep water. I didn't know what it was supposed to mean or how it fit in with the other things we were studying, but I just felt really excited that somebody thought it was important.

I only had random ideas, like taking a tape recorder and a mic with me the next time I went to the farm with the compost bucket. I didn't have money for many long-distance calls and Amy and I decided to send a tape of us talking back and forth. It was my turn now with the tape and I thought I'd get chicken squawking for ambiance.

When I got there the wind was kicking up and blowing my hair all over, but I didn't have an elastic so I put it in a braid. My hair was long, almost to my butt, and curly, so if I braided it to the very ends it would stay. Amy used to say it looked like a black whip when I did that, and like I could kill someone with it.

I wasn't doing very well with the chicken sounds though because of the wind, and also because the white-haired farm guy and another guy, a young guy, were hammering and sawing on the backside of the barn. I turned off the tape recorder and waited. Maybe it was stupid, but I really wanted those damn chickens squawking on the tape. I was having one of my homesick days, even though I wasn't longing for any particular place or missing a person, except maybe Amy. I just had days when I felt ragged like that.

For a while when I was a kid and had to wait for the school bus or something I'd go through the forms I was learning in my karate class, because I used to love those. Sitting there staring at the chickens, I tried running through one in my mind and using my hands to see if I could remember. I used to know a lot of the forms too, because I'd started karate when I was eleven and kept it up until I was fourteen.

So, there I was at the farm in a clump of grass by the chicken coop doing miniature *haito*'s and *shuto*'s with my hands and the young guy walked by with a couple of two-by-fours balanced on his shoulder. He glanced over at me and kept walking. My face got all hot when I realized he must have seen my faux karate because I probably looked deranged and carpenters are always kind of cool, with their big tool belts and everything. It was like when I was a kid and I used to have all these little hand tricks I invented myself, and when my mom caught me practicing she always said that I looked like I had just walked out of a mental institution.

* * *

A couple of days later I decided to go back, thinking I'd try one more time to record the chickens, but the carpentry was still going on so I recorded those noises instead. The joke at the college was that you could do just about anything for credit, and I hoped the equipment made me at least look like I was doing a school project, especially when the carpenter got a big drill out of the back of a van and he passed nearby me again. I figured he was a student too. He looked it, with his flannel shirt and jeans, and hair cut in a kind of grown-out Mohawk, with a bit of a beard. Actually, his hair was kind of like mine, curly and dark, except for the cut. I expected him to ignore me, but suddenly he goes, "Was that sign language you were doing the other day?" He was standing there with his shoulders kind of tilted, and he was pretty good-looking to tell the truth.

I got all flustered and said, "Uh, no. I was just trying to remember something." And I thought, *Oh, yes, that will clear it up.* But he nodded and smiled this really warm smile that made his eyes crinkle up at the corners. Then he took the drill and went back to work, and I fled before I'd have the chance to say or do some other ridiculous thing.

2

Going to sleep that night I was restless. That old, familiar ache started acting up again, the kind of ache that makes even a small bed feel too empty, and my bed was always empty.

When I was a kid the pleasures of the flesh were all about ice cream or trampolines or getting to hold your friend's pet rabbit, but by the time I was twelve all that had started to change. I became fascinated by kissing, as if my lips had come to life and had desires all their own. Then when I was thirteen and seriously liked a boy for the first time, kissing was all I thought about.

Noah was this blond-headed kid in my karate class who went to a different middle school and we always paired up for sit-ups and stretching, and after class I'd imagine us lying on a couch or a bed and kissing the night away. And I could imagine tongues on necks and things like that, but I didn't know how you might cross the divide from a karate class to a couch in the dark, and the weeks and months passed by and I'd just be sick with longing.

If when I was twelve my lips came to life, by the time I was in the middle of high school all my body parts ached. I don't know how it normally happens, but I remember the first moment when the idea of actual sex became appealing. I was sixteen, at Amy's house, and there was this pot of very penile cactuses on the porch. I looked at them, and, Bling! A lightbulb popped on. And that's when the real agony started, because I knew I'd really have to like a boy to want to have sex with him, and the fulfillment of all that desire would depend on the spontaneous occurrence of a mutual attraction, and the chances of that happening were about a billion to one.

It wasn't all random odds either, because right from the get-go I had a knack for ruining my chances. By the time I'd quit karate, in tenth grade, Noah and I were going to the same high school and I was living with my dad in town in an apartment complex behind a Payless. One night, Valentine's Day, I was at home alone talking to Amy on the phone, and there was a knock at the door. Noah's older brother and his girlfriend were standing there, and they said they'd brought a present from Noah. It was a big chocolate heart and a card with pictures of strawberries on it with a caption that read, *There's so much to like about you*, and signed with Noah's name, and even though I'd liked him for so long I suddenly felt like I was going to throw up.

I didn't want to take the chocolate heart and the card, and I told them to tell Noah that I liked someone else, but his brother said, "Just take it, he asked us to give them to you." They left and I was shaking all over. I shoved the card and the heart way deep down in the trash can in the kitchen where my dad would never see them and I got back on the phone with Amy, and just felt insanely nauseous.

Amy said, "He's cute, though. You should go for it!"

I couldn't even get my mind around what I was so scared of, but "going for it" with Noah just seemed out of the question, and then it wasn't all that long before Noah was going out with another girl, and I did like someone else, a boy named Hector Alvarez.

One time during that year this crazy kid in my journalism class made a list of the fifty girls he considered the most attractive, in order of attractiveness, and tacked it up in the newspaper room. Everyone read the list, even though we all thought it was weird he did it, but Amy was appalled. She looked like she was going to rip it off the wall. Then she sat down and made a list of fifty guys and passed it around to a bunch of girls, saying we needed a little equal opportunity. We rated the guys anonymously, according to a point system based on how far we would go with them, and when it was my turn I gave most of them zeros. I didn't do it to be mean or anything, I just didn't find them appealing, even in theory when there was nothing real to scare me off.

The only clear winner, when Amy did the tally, was Hector because another girl and I both liked him and we both gave him the top rating. We were in art class when Amy added up the numbers and the teacher, Mr. MacLeod, was over in the pottery room talking to Mr. Knight, the pottery teacher. Mr. MacLeod had his groupies, and Mr. Knight had his, and the two classrooms shared this patio, and Hector, who was a Mr. Knight groupie, often worked out there. Amy and I and our other friends were MacLeod groupies, and one time, the week before, when Hector was out on the patio working on a sculpture, I tried to get up the nerve to go talk to him.

I'd already liked him for months, but it was pretty much from afar. I could tell he was nice, and he was good at pottery and rode a skateboard in that super fluid way some guys do, and mostly I just thought he was extremely good-looking. That day on the patio I didn't know what to say, so I just went and sat on the cement wall that ran around the patio, near to where he was working, and tried to check out the sculpture.

After a little while, Hector goes, "Did you see them?"

I had on a band shirt, a reggae band from the Bay Area, and I said, "Yeah," and that was it. The whole conversation. Girls at school were all the time talking freely with guys and flirting their heads off but I was about as naturally able in that area as I was in a gym class softball game where I never once hit the ball. Later, when Amy told him that he got the top rating in our game he just thought it was a weird joke. He wasn't all full of himself, which was another reason I liked him, but my inability to hold up a conversation was definitely a strike against me.

There were two times at parties back then that I took the Vodka Express and made out with guys I didn't actually like. I did it because they weren't repulsive, and they made the moves, and I was drunk, but only drunk enough to have the excuse of being drunk so I wouldn't have to talk to them again. I did it because I was desperate to get physical with a guy, and get some experience, but the fact that I didn't actually like them made the whole thing ridiculous. I knew it had to be different if you truly liked the guy, and after the second one, I decided that until there was a guy that I really did like, there wouldn't be any action for me. And maybe that decision saved me a measure of ridiculosity, but it never did anything to relieve the agony.

* * *

The next day at Media Loan there was a big rush with patrons lining up all the way from the desks to the door picking up equipment or returning it. When things settled down, and Calvin and I were in the back putting stuff away, I said, "Calvin, how important do you think sex is? I mean, in life."

And he goes, "What, like on a scale from one to ten?"

"Sure."

He thought for a second. "I don't know... maybe between... seventy and eighty?"

I laughed. "Oh."

"What about you? I mean, aren't there times where," he brought his voice down to a whisper, "you just want to fuck and fuck..."

My face got hot. "I'm not saying." Then I said, "What about love? Same scale."

And Calvin goes, "What's love got to do with it?" And he started singing, "*Oh-o-o-oh, what's love got-ta-do, got-ta-do with it...*" He quieted down and slipped the cable he was wrapping off his elbow. He said, "I was in love once."

"A guy in Seattle?"

"No, actually, it was a guy in my hometown. Total secret. Then it ended and I thought I was going to die."

"Oh, man."

Calvin sighed. "But life goes on, you know. And Seattle was pretty soon after that, and then I decided to come to this crazy place."

I set a stack of mic boxes on a shelf. "Are you glad you came here?"

"For sure, aren't you?"

I said definitely, but there were two things I could wish for, and he said, "Well?"

I said, "More sun."

"And?"

"You know."

And he goes, "Right. Well, join the club." After a minute he said, "Anyone around here caught your eye?"

I thought about it. There were definitely a few good-looking guys around. There was this guy named Tyler in my multicultural literature class who was pretty nice to look at, but I didn't know him at all, and I thought of that carpenter from the farm, but I really didn't know him.

I said, "No. What about you?"

Calvin sighed, "Not at the moment." Then he said, "I wouldn't worry too much if I were you, though. You're bound to meet someone soon, you're adorable."

I said, "God, you're so nice."

And he said, "Sister, just telling it like it is."

* * *

I went back to the farm a few days later and it was quiet and not windy and no one else was around. It would have been the perfect time to record the chickens but I didn't care anymore. My chicken moment had passed and I was kind of disappointed the carpenter guy wasn't there. Maybe I could have had the chance to say something ridiculous, I wouldn't have minded. I walked over to where they'd been working. A new section of the barn wall was freshly painted and stood out next to the rest of it, and I dug a little trail through a patch of sawdust with my shoe.

I remembered his eyes and the angle of his shoulders when he asked me what I'd been doing, and I wished I could have seen his smile again.

3

Even though we were next-door roommates, Renee and I didn't exactly connect right away. At first, she was always rushing off to a class or a meeting or work, or going down to Portland for the weekend, and she had friends she got together with to throw boomerangs, who were all sort of hip and sporty and didn't seem like my kind of crowd. Plus, she could be a little bit rude.

One day when I was reading she came in my room to get the phone. It was on this long cord attached to the jack in her room, and she picked it up off the floor, looked around, and said, "You have too many things on your walls." I guess I was pretty sensitive about that sort of thing, I'll admit that, because what you put on your walls is a very personal choice, you may as well have your whole personality up there, and I didn't know how to answer her. I never do when someone says something I think is rude, I just fume about it and come up with the right answer about twenty hours later. So, I sat there and kept reading, and she left to go make her phone call.

But then this one night we were both in the bathroom, because there were two sinks, and this really big mirror over the whole counter, and we started making funny faces and then invented a dance for bucktoothed rabbits and pretty soon we were both dying of laughter. At one point, she put her hair up in this big balloon bun on top of her head. Her hair wasn't as long as mine, but it was pretty long, and wavy and reddish brown, and that bun thing looked like a beehive hair-do, and I said, "That look is stunning."

And she goes, "Ain't it though?" And then she looked at herself close up in the mirror and said, "God, I look pale next to you."

I said, "I think it's just my freckles."

* * *

After that night, any time Renee needed to get the phone from my room when I was in there she'd hang around a few minutes to talk. Other times we'd make dinner together or go eat at The Corner, this little food place in the building with all the laundry machines, where you could get a good old hippie meal for cheap. Often we stayed up late lounging on her bed if her boyfriend, Alec, wasn't visiting. I was getting to know Alec too, he was sweet and quite funny. They'd been together forever, two years.

When Renee first told me she was from Berkeley, I said I was too, partially, just when I was little. One afternoon we were taking a study break at the apartment, sitting on the kitchen counter drinking tea, and she asked me what street I lived on in Berkeley.

I said, "Streets, plural."

"Like?"

I took one hand off my tea cup to count the places on my fingers. "Yeah, Arch Street, Blake, Belvedere, California, Acton...that's it."

She asked me what schools I went to, and I asked her the same, and then I told her about going to Hebrew school for a year or two at a temple on Vine Street or somewhere. My memories of Berkeley weren't always clear.

She said, "I knew you were Jewish."

"Did you?"

"Totally."

She said she knew the temple I meant but she'd never been there because her mom wasn't religious at all, too Bohemian. I said same with my mom. Same with my dad. Hebrew school was his idea, but aside from that I'd grown up entirely secular.

Renee said she grew up with a lot of tradition though, holidays and Friday night dinners with her grandparents and aunt and cousins.

I had no idea what that would be like, but I said, "That must be cozy," because it did sound cozy. Actually, I tended to be a little jealous of that sort of thing.

She said, "You should come sometime."

That night I had this crazy dream that Renee and I were in a band together, and played for some kid's bar mitzvah. It was a punk band called Kosher Chicken Vagina. That's right. Kosher. Chicken. Vagina. And in the morning when I told her she laughed for about half an hour. A couple of our other roommates were there and they just looked at me like I was insane.

* * *

Another person I knew with a lot of tradition in their life was my friend Hari. I'd met him the year before, after high school graduation, when I moved to Marin to stay with an old friend of my dad's and work at a food co-op. I needed to earn money but I thought I'd die if I stayed in Ukiah.

All my friends had left Ukiah. Amy was in San Francisco taking classes at City College, and every Friday afternoon I took a bus over the Golden Gate and spent the weekend with her. One Saturday we went to this yoga workshop at a studio near her apartment. Yoga was her new thing, and this was kundalini style, which neither of us had ever heard of.

The workshop started off with meditation and chanting, and then got very vigorous with a lot of fast movements and heavy breathing, and I don't think I was coordinating very well because at one point I thought I was going to hyperventilate. Thankfully though we started the cool down and I was saved. After that the instructor had us do this exercise where you got a partner and took turns talking about peace in your life, how you found peace or connected to it, and you were supposed to get with a person in the room you didn't know. Then before I started panicking about who I'd pair up with, the guy next to me said, "Hey, I'm Hari."

He had on a tank top and these billowy white pants, and long hair that was tied up in a knot on the top of his head with a white cloth wound around it, and he looked about my age.

I said, "I'm Talia."

Then the instructor rang a bell to get started and I said, "Do you want to go first? You kind of look like an expert in this." I'd been noticing his perfect yoga all morning.

He laughed, "Not quite." Then he looked around the room and said, "Well, I don't usually talk about this kind of stuff right away, not with people I don't know, but I guess you look nice." He said he was a Sikh and that his family was pretty observant, and in terms of feeling peaceful, he felt very connected to his creator, especially when he did his morning practices, which helped him set a tone for the whole day.

He said, "Feeling connected really guides me. I depend on it for pretty much all my decisions."

Hari had this very calm, gentle voice, and he seemed very sincere. There are people who like to make a big show of how spiritual they are, but he wasn't like that. He wasn't like anyone I'd ever met.

The instructor rang the little bell, meaning it was time to switch, and I said I didn't have any practice or tradition like he had but I kind of wished I did.

I said, "I don't know if I actually feel peaceful that often." I told him I could think of instances, but not anything that happened on a regular basis.

Hari said, "Okay, so like what's an example?"

I said, "Maybe seeing something really beautiful, like when the sun goes down on a clear evening in winter, and you see black tree branches against the sky."

"That sounds pretty peaceful."

"Or like last year, in school, in art class, I had a week where I was working on a painting, and I got so absorbed in it, it was like I'd forget about the time completely. I forgot *myself*. That hardly ever happens."

He nodded.

Then I said, "But I guess those things are different. They don't compare to feeling connected to your creator."

And Hari said, "I don't agree."

* * *

During the lunch break we sat together. Amy asked Hari if he lived in the neighborhood and he said no, he lived in Los Angeles, he was just up visiting his aunt and uncle for the weekend, he tried to see them a couple times a year at least. Then we talked about school—he had just started at UCLA—and what we did for fun besides yoga workshops. After lunch, there was a guided meditation session and then the workshop was over, and after we packed up, Hari and Amy and I stood out on the sidewalk saying goodbye.

He said it was really great to meet us and I wanted to ask him if he might want to exchange addresses so that maybe we could keep in touch, maybe talk more about peace. I really wanted to, but I chickened out. And then he said he had to run, he was meeting his aunt and uncle, and he said take care, and he went jogging down the hill.

Amy said, "What a sweetheart."

I didn't tell her I'd wanted to ask for his address. I didn't want her to tell me I should have, because I felt bad enough already.

* * *

But then on Monday the weirdest thing happened. I had the opening shift at work and just as I was wiping down the counter at one of the cash registers, a customer came in.

It was Hari.

We stared at each other for a second, and then he said, "I can't believe it."

I said, "Me neither."

"You work here?" I was wearing an apron and a name tag. It was obvious. He said, "My aunt and uncle live like half a mile from here."

"No way."

"They're just taking me to the bus station right now. They're out in the car." He held up a finger. "I'll be right back."

A minute later he was back with a bag of apples and a bottle of juice, and I blurted out, "Do you want to exchange addresses?" And then I was horrified I'd said it, because he'd think I was some freakish loser, like I was trying to latch onto him after meeting him for only a few hours.

But he said, "I was going to ask you that."

4

That thing with Hari at the store, or the day of the rainbows, I wanted to tell you about those because maybe in a way I still believe in magic. I guess it's the same with why I always had special feelings for Halloween. I mean, all kids do because of the candy and everything, but when I got older I still loved it. My favorite picture book when I was little was *Where the Wild Things Are*, because I loved how Max's room dissolved into a forest, even though he was being punished, and took him to that other land. Ordinary things became suddenly magical and I always thought Halloween was like that.

This year it was on a Friday. Alec drove up from Portland and he and Renee went over to the athletic field across from our building with the boomerang crowd to practice throwing. Renee asked me if I wanted to try, and I said okay, and she started showing me how to throw and how to catch, but in the end I couldn't deal with a piece of spinning wood flying at my face. I told her I wanted to take a break and sat in the grass near the walking path.

Halloween was already starting to cast its spell. The boomerangs were whipping out over the field, a clump of vampires sauntered by and a girl on a bike swooshed past with a shark fin on her back. Another handful of people were whooping across the other end of the field going, "The Freak Show is coming!" and a kid with bare feet kept flying by on a skateboard with his long hair and velvet cape trailing out behind him. More and more people were coming out, and it was all very Hieronymous Bosch, like the painting my dad had hanging over the couch my whole life. Wherever he lived he had that painting and that couch. When I was little we used to sit there while he read *Where the Wild Things Are* to me, and I'd look at the pictures and at the painting, and they just kind of merged.

So, I was sitting there in the grass, hugging my knees and starting to feel hypnotized, and just as a stray boomerang landed near me I saw Calvin and his roommate Toby heading in my direction. They weren't dressed up for Halloween but they made a nice pair, with tall, skinny Calvin in his customary black leather jacket with a lot of zippers and his black hair flipped to one side. Toby was shorter and stockier, with his auburn combo of slight goatee and heavy eyebrows, and hair sticking out from under his backwards baseball cap.

Calvin goes, "Hey girl, what's up?" I said not much and asked what they were doing, and Toby said they were going to walk down to the beach. Calvin zipped up the main zipper on his jacket, "You don't look like you're doing anything, why don't you come?"

When I told Renee I was going, Alec said, "Ren, let's go too. I never get to go to the beach anymore."

The sun was just dipping down below the tops of the cedars, and we crossed the road into the forest to find one of the trails that led down to the beach. It was cold and dusky in the trees, and the path wound through them, forking occasionally, and when we passed by a big tree that had a handful of boards nailed to it, Renee and Alec and Toby wanted to stop and climb it. Calvin and I stayed on the ground, and while we were waiting Calvin asked me if I'd heard about Bob, since the legend of that forest was that Bob was this giant metal ball that rolled around of its own accord.

I said, "Are you joking?"

And he goes, "No, people have actually seen it." And when this started to blow my mind, the climbers dropped down from the tree. Plop! Plop! Plop! Toby was a second-year student, like Calvin, and Calvin said to him, "You've seen Bob, right?"

Toby said, "Twice, in different spots, but not this year so far."

This was so weird to me. "Really?"

Alec said, "Everybody knows Bob down at Reed." But then he laughed. "Who's Bob?"

We all started walking again, further down the trail to where the ground sloped because we were getting closer to the beach.

When we broke out of the trees the last of the day's light was glinting over the water. It was so wide and open after being in the forest. The edge of the land curved away in both directions with soft little green waves lapping the shore, and we all sprawled out on a patch of coarse sand full of tiny seashells. The first stars started to come out, and right then everyone looked to me like a bunch of barnacles on a rock, and I had this weird thought out of nowhere that we weren't actually individuals, as if the fading light didn't just wipe out our facial features, but our personalities too.

I leaned over to Calvin and said, "Isn't it scary that we aren't individuals?"

And he goes, "Are you on something?" I said no, it was just a thought.

Renee said, "Don't mind her, she's full of strange ideas."

Calvin put a hand on my shoulder and said, "Well, just face your humanity."

I laughed and flung handfuls of shells into the starlit water. I felt good sitting there with everyone. I was finally starting to feel like I had people I was connected to. I hadn't hung out with Toby before, but he was really friendly. He was sitting next to me, and he threw a rock far out into the water, way past where my shells had gone. Then he kind of cracked his neck and looked at me. "So, what's your thing?"

I said, "Art, pretty much." Art had always been my thing, even though it wasn't my focus in school now. I wanted to study history and literature and a lot of things.

Toby said, "That's cool."

"Yeah, art's her thing," Calvin said. "She did the drawing for the Media Loan t-shirts I made."

And Toby goes, "Oh yeah, I wanted one of those, but Calvin didn't have enough."

I was pretty flattered by that. I asked Toby what his thing was and he said music, and that he was starting to get into experimental composition. Calvin goes, "He's good too. He's wicked on guitar."

Renee said, "You sound like you're trying to set them up."

"I'm totally not," Calvin said. "Toby's already spoken for. Right Bro? Me and Talia are the only ones here that are single and carefree."

All this was making me need to cough in the worst way, like I did when something was embarrassing, but then Renee goes, "Yeah, and Talia's still waiting to get deflowered."

I felt my face burst into flames. I pictured it setting my hair on fire in a big halo, and for a second I just waited for my soul to exit my body. There was dead silence. Then I heard Alec say, "Renee..."

And Calvin said, "I think we should get going, it's getting dark."

Actually, it was very dark, almost pitch black once we got up into the trees again. No one had thought to bring a flashlight so we formed a human chain to make sure we stayed together. I grabbed Calvin's hand, and then Alec's, because I wasn't going to hold Renee's. Right then I would have preferred being lost alone in the forest.

We staggered along in single file, with Toby at the front.

After a while, Calvin goes, "Toby, are you sure we're going the right way?"

Toby had a pack of matches and we stopped while he lit one. There was a brief flicker of light while he looked quickly in both directions on the path, trying to suss things out before the flame burned his fingers.

Calvin thought we should change directions because there was a fork he didn't recognize, so we did, and kept going, stopping at intervals to light matches until we all started getting pretty confused.

I was too lost to even be confused. My legs were tired and I had a rock in my shoe and in between the matches the only visible thing was a trail of sky up above the trees, only the tiniest bit paler than the absolute dark. It seemed like we'd been walking for hours, so long in the dark I started wondering if this was what it was like to be blind. I kept imagining Bob the metal ball rolling out of the forest and squashing us, which seemed like a fitting end for Halloween, complete with the special irony of me getting killed without even having been deflowered first. Or maybe Bob would only squash Renee, and that would be my personal poetic justice.

Finally, on the fifth or sixth match I had this very metaphysical idea, that speed would override those moments of deliberation and break us out of the puzzle we were in.

"If we just go fast enough," I said, "the momentum will carry us through the confusion."

Toby goes, "Wow."

Calvin goes, "You *are* on something."

But then Alec said, "You guys, I think I see a light up there."

"Let's go," Toby said, picking up the pace.

Ten minutes later a road became visible through the trees and we made it to the outskirts of campus. The blindfold of the night was off, a relief, and after I got the rock out of my stupid shoe I remembered I was still upset with Renee, and I started ignoring her when she tried to talk to me.

When we were passing through a loading dock, she caught my arm, waited until the others were ahead of us, and said, "Are you mad at me?" When I didn't answer right away she said, "I'm an asshole sometimes." She stuffed her hands in her pockets. "Sorry."

"You really didn't need to shout out my personal information," I said. "In front of people."

And she goes, "You're right."

"Why'd you even say it in the first place?"

She thought about it a minute. "I guess I like to tease people."

"I guess."

We stood there a minute, and then she kind of punched my arm. "Let's go see the freak show, okay?" We'd been heading up toward Red Square, but I'd been thinking maybe I'd just go home.

I punched her arm back, maybe a tad harder, and said, "Okay, let's."

We ran to catch up with the guys, and I started thinking maybe the night wasn't wrecked after all. I told myself I'd have to remember that momentum and confusion thing. I knew Alec was studying physics and thought maybe he could help me write it up in an equation.

* * *

A few weeks after that it was Renee's birthday. That night I gave her a mix tape I'd made, with collaged letters on the cover that spelled out Kosher Chicken Vagina, and she put it on the stereo. Alec was up from Portland again and several of Renee's boomerang friends came by. Our other roommates brought out their music, and pretty soon there was a party going on. We pushed back all the furniture so people could dance, and all those bodies moving really started heating the place up. I'd loved to dance in high school and it had been a long time since I'd had the chance, but once I got going it was just great to move again.

The windows of the apartment were at ground level and we often used them as doors, and at one point, when I was overheating from dancing I stepped outside to get some air, I saw Tyler, that cute guy from my multicultural literature class. He was going by on the walking path with a backpack on, like he'd just come from a late night at the library, and he spotted me standing there outside the window.

I said hello, and he stopped walking. "It's Talia, right?"

I nodded and pointed at him, "Tyler?" even though I knew very well what his name was.

He stood out in the class because he was older than most of the group, twenty-two or twenty-three, not a boy but a man. Plus, he was tall and angular and cool, and sounded very mature and confident when he made comments in class. I wondered what he was doing down by the dorms at night because I'd assumed he lived off campus.

He tromped over to the window from the path. He smiled, "Is this your place?"

"It is."

"Looks like quite a party."

I was all warm and loose and springy from dancing, and I heard myself say, "Feel like coming in?" And he shocked me by saying sure, and when we stepped inside through the window someone handed him a beer. It turned out he knew a couple of the boomerang guys and they started talking and I got back to dancing, but pretty soon I realized Tyler and I were kind of dancing together.

I hadn't connected with him in class at all. He wasn't unfriendly, just sort of aloof, but now I was getting a different vibe. Nothing crazy, but he was smiling and I was smiling and I started getting light-headed. His moves were sort of understated, but you could see he got the music and I kept staring at his hair because of how thick it was. It was sandy-colored and cut short so it stuck straight up on the top and I started thinking he'd need a miniature lawn mower to cut it, and I kind of started laughing because I can get a little manic when I dance. Renee was in reach and I grabbed her arm and we started doing this goofy weird rabbit dance we'd invented that first night we made faces in the bathroom mirror, and if I'd had any hopes of looking cool in front of Tyler I knew I'd blown it. But right at that second I didn't care because Renee and I were laughing too much.

We quit the rabbit thing and resumed regular dancing and right then Tyler leaned down and said in my ear, "I like how you dance." His eyes were right up close, brown specks in the blue, and I was too startled to say "thanks" or "you too" or something else that might have been normal. A minute later he said he was supposed to meet a friend and should get going, and then he said,

"Now that I know where you live, I'll stop by sometime."

I said, "Cool."

It was cool. Definitely not what I expected.

* * *

The next morning, I was rinsing and crushing cans for the recycling in the kitchen and Renee came in from cleaning the bathroom and she goes, "What's up with that Tyler guy?" And I asked her what she meant, and she goes, "He was acting hella into you." I looked up at her to see if she was joking, and she was kind of smiling but I could tell she was serious.

"What? I don't think so." I hadn't wanted to assume anything, get my hopes up for nothing.

"You don't?"

"I guess he did say he liked the way I danced. And that he might stop by."

"See?"

"Does that sound flirty to you?"

"Talia."

I laughed. "You know I'm not used to this kind of thing."

And she goes, "Yeah, well get used to it. Maybe you'll finally get some."

"Would you please shut up?" I was starting to get those bees in my stomach. "You don't even know if I'd be interested in him."

And she goes, "Yes I do."

5

On Monday, I was about ten minutes early to multicultural literature. It was the last week of classes for the term and I kept looking up when anyone came in, expecting to see Tyler, but it got later and later and it didn't seem like he was going to show. Then, just as the professor was shutting the door Tyler walked in and sat across the room in the last empty seat. He saw me and smiled, and gave a little wave by sort of cocking his flat hand to one side. I smiled back and then stared at my notebook. The professor was reviewing the requirements for the final papers and taking questions, and before I knew it class was over.

I was closer to the door than Tyler was and kind of took my time getting my stuff in my backpack, and then he was standing right there saying, "How's it going?"

"Good." And then I even managed to say, "Nice to see you the other night."

He smiled, "That was fun." Then he asked me which book I was writing my paper on, and we walked out to

Red Square talking about the books we'd chosen, until he said he had to get to his shift at work, downtown.

The next day after class it was pretty much the same. We talked for a few minutes and then he said he was off to his banjo lesson.

I said, "Banjo?"

"Yeah." He played a moment of air banjo and I laughed. He looked like he was pretty good at it.

I asked him how long he'd been taking lessons and he said only a few months. We were out in Red Square again and he glanced up at the clock tower. "See you Thursday?"

"For sure."

I watched him jog away toward the stairs to the bus roundabout. It was twilight already and everything was blue, except the globes of the lampposts, which had come on and glowed yellow. And it was cold. I put up the hood of my parka and for a second I thought there was a swarm of moths around the nearest lamppost, but then I felt pricking on my cheeks and I realized it was snowing. Pretty soon the square was all dusted over, and mostly deserted, and I walked around, scooting my feet and making dark tracks in the blue-white snow dust.

Tyler was being very congenial, but I wasn't so sure he liked me like Renee thought. I mean, it didn't matter, I barely knew him. He was pretty disgustingly good-looking though, I had to admit that. And it was cool how he was learning banjo, and said smart things in class, and worked at a restaurant with a bar where the tips were good. I walked around for a while, watching the layer of snow on the ground getting a tiny bit thicker and a tiny bit thicker.

That night instead of a bout of agony I felt another kind of restlessness, more like anticipation. And when the bed started to feel too empty, I thought about Tyler--the angular lines of his jaw and shoulders, his spiky hair, and his soft-looking lips--and I did it for myself, touched myself, because sometimes there is just no other remedy.

* * *

It snowed more through the night and into the next day. I had my other classes and papers to write and a shift at Media Loan, but I hadn't been in the snow that many times and it was pretty mesmerizing, so I kept going outside to walk around. About noon I passed by this couple, a guy and a girl, making out in front of the library building, and they were so passionate they fell over into a snowbank and kept right on going, and people passing by told them to get a room.

The sun came out late in the afternoon, just in time to go down, and filled the snow full of pink and blue shadows. And it was all so beautiful, but I wasn't feeling peaceful at all. At the very end of the day, on my way home, I saw Calvin's roommate, Toby, and his girlfriend out on the athletic field having a romantic little snowball fight, and I started to feel like it was all a bit too much. I thought how it must be pretty wonderful to have a person you were that close to, how as much as I loved my friends there was nothing there that quenched that ache. Maybe I didn't completely understand it, but the feeling was so keen it clawed right through me. Like I was always reaching for something I could never get to and my hands always came up empty. Other people paired up so easily. I wondered what their secret was.

* * *

Thursday literature class was the last of the term. When it was over, Tyler and I walked outside together, and I said, "Are you off to work?"

"Not today."

"Banjo lesson?"

"Nope."

"Dog show?" Wow, wasn't I being witty.

He laughed, "Not this week."

We stood there a second and then he said, "Are you walking that way?" He tilted his head toward the stairs that led past the college activities building and eventually toward the residential area. I said yes, and he said, "I'll walk with you."

I asked him what he was doing for winter break and he said working mostly, but also going to see his family in Anacortes. He said our literature class was his last class, probably ever. He had a couple projects to finish up in the spring, but then he'd have enough credits to graduate.

When we got to my building I saw Renee through the windows banging around in the kitchen, and I asked Tyler if he wanted to come in. I said it very casually, or tried to, even though I suddenly felt like my voice box had become dislodged and I was working myself like a puppet. But he said sure and I was even more surprised than the night of the party.

Renee looked up when we came in and she said, "Tal, spaghetti. Do you have anything I can use in a sauce?" I had mushrooms and onions, and pretty soon the three of us were cooking, and the windows steamed up and the air got thick with the smell of olive oil and bay leaves. Renee asked Tyler how he knew her boomerang friends and they started talking about that and it was a relief to have help moving the conversation along. She had Fleetwood Mac on the stereo and cooking kept my hands busy, and even though I didn't have ideas about what was going to happen beyond dinner that feeling of anticipation came back very strong.

I liked how Tyler looked eating, at ease with his elbows on the table, and smiling when he caught me looking at him. He and Renee talked about working at the photo lab, since he used to work there too, and then we talked about the best and worst jobs we'd all had, and he said his favorite was one summer when he worked for a canoe rental place because he could take the canoes out any time he wanted.

After we finished eating Renee started getting ready to go up to the computer lab to work on a paper, and our other roommates were coming and going. I kept expecting Tyler to say he had to take off, but he offered to help me with the dishes and he stood very close while I washed and he rinsed. Our hands kept bumping together while we passed the dishes and adjusted the water, and at one point when he wiped a blob of suds off my arm with his fingers I thought my arm was going to faint.

We were talking about music and he asked me what kinds I liked.

I said, "A lot of kinds, but lately I've been pretty obsessed with the Velvet Underground." I fished out a handful of forks from the water. "What about you?"

"I'm really into bluegrass these days. Banjo and all." He took the forks from me and smiled.

The dishes were done and I let the water out and we started drying our hands. I said, "The closest thing to bluegrass I'm into is Camper Van Beethoven. I mean, it's not bluegrass at all but they do have a violin player."

He said, "Do you have a record of theirs you can play me?"

Which is how we ended up in my room with the door closed.

He sat next to me on the floor with his long legs folded up, and we talked and listened to the whole Camper Van album, and all the while I sensed this pressure building up between us. And then I put on the Velvet Underground, and I said, "Do you like them?" All I had was this second-hand boom box, but the sound was pretty decent.

He goes, "Mm hmm," moving his head to the music. "You have a lot of pictures on your walls." I thought again, *Too many?* I wondered what his bedroom looked like, a place in town, with just an art poster or two, probably, and his banjo standing up in the corner.

"I must seem like a kid to you."

He looked at me, and I saw the brown flecks in his blue eyes and the black of his pupils, and I felt hot in my throat and down my spine.

He goes, "Yeah, kinda. It's sweet though." And he slipped a hand into my hair and touched the nape of my neck with his long fingers, and he said, "You're so pretty."

And he leaned forward, his sandy-colored eyelashes coming closer, and his mouth just a bit open and Bang! That invisible barrier broke. His mouth was on mine, his lips pressing soft and warm and the tip of his tongue flicking. He held the back of my head and the kiss went deeper, and I put my hand on his shoulder and grabbed a handful of his shirt. Then, still kissing, we moved to the bed.

I felt his short, thick hair under my hands and his shoulder blades under his t-shirt, and a hard bulge in his pants when we pressed together. His breathing got heavy and then his hands were under my shirt, and mine were under his, and I touched his stomach and the hair on his chest.

And this continued on until he pulled back and rubbed his thumb over his lips. "Are you a virgin?"

My cheeks were raw from his sandpapery chin, and I was kind of breathless, but I said, "Can you tell?"

And he said, "I don't want us to do anything you'll regret."

I said, "I'm feeling good about this."

He laughed. Then he sat up and reached toward the lamp on the night table. "Mind if I turn this off?"

"No."

The blind was down over the window but the edges glowed from the snow and the closest lamppost, and I couldn't really see his face just his general shape, and all of sudden I had that Where-the-Wild-Things-Are feeling, like the walls were melting into forest, because we were kissing again and taking our clothes off, and then he asked me if I had any protection.

I had a little candy-colored stash of condoms in the night table drawer. You could get them for free all over campus, along with safe sex pamphlets, and I took a few now and then because I did think, *Well, someday*, even though I never thought it would be *today*, which was completely surreal. I got one out and handed it to him. I didn't know what to do next but I was sure he'd been with lots of girls and I could follow his lead.

I lay back on the bed. I heard him tear the wrapper, and a minute later he moved over me so that his bare belly touched mine, and our chests and legs touched. It was so much skin, I never realized I had so much skin, and that other people had so much skin. Being naked together was a whole thing in itself, way more wild and exciting than I would have guessed. And even then it was still a prelude to what was coming next, because he started maneuvering between my legs, and I opened them, and he started to put it in.

I felt this sharp little pain and sucked in my breath, and he backed off for a second and then tried again. And then he was fully in me, and started moving. It hurt less after a minute, and by then he was going in more of a rhythm and I started to relax into it.

I put my arms around his shoulders and then slid them down to his waist, and because of his weight and the movement and the pressure my breathing was coming out in a kind of panting. I didn't know if we were dancing or wrestling or swimming or what but it was like all of that at once. And then he was going faster, and breathing harder, and I held onto him tighter. All at once he held his breath and kind of strained, and pushed in deeper, and then let out a big gasp of air, collapsing down on me with his mouth by my ear. My heart was still drumming and I put my hand on the back of his neck.

Then he rolled over on his back. "You okay?"

"Yeah." I was in a daze.

"You sure?"

"Yeah. Yeah, it's just new territory for me."

He found my hand and squeezed it.

* * *

When Tyler left, it was about two in the morning. We'd been lying in the dark, and he touched my cheek and he said, "Hey, I'd better go."

I said, "Okay."

He said, "You're really sweet."

We sat up and he cupped my face in his hands and kissed me on the lips, not the hungry kind of kiss like before, but a quiet one, a good-bye one. He said he had a lot of work he had to get to the next day, and then a shift at the restaurant, but I wasn't too concerned with his reasons for going, actually I was relieved. I didn't think I'd sleep a lot with him in the bed with me, and just then I was pretty tired, and, more than that, I'd just done this thing I'd never ever done, and even though I'd imagined it a thousand times the real thing was different, and it was like I was scattered around the room like my clothes were.

After he left I straightened out the blankets and put on pajamas and lay down in the bed. I touched my arms and legs, and my face, and between my legs, and my body hummed. It hummed like it was singing a song, and slowly I got sleepy and finally I drifted off.

* * *

I woke up late, after eleven in the morning. I drank a big glass of water and felt it whooshing down my insides, and then I took a shower and the water whooshed the outsides. As I was drying off and getting dressed, I kept thinking, *I had sex. I had sex with Tyler. I am sexually active.*

Around noon I was sitting at the table eating toast and reading when Renee came in all sweaty from a workout at the rec center. She was heading for the shower, but she pointed at me and said, "I want a report when I'm done," and I smiled and said okay.

Twenty minutes later she was sitting next to me on a chair, in her brown bathrobe, with a towel around her head, and she said, "Okay. How was your night?"

I said, "Interesting."

She grabbed my wrist and opened her eyes wide. "What did you do?" But obviously, she already knew. She dragged me into her room and shut the door.

"How do you feel?"

I smiled, "Pretty good."

"Okay."

"Kind of initiated."

She laughed. Then she said, "Did he sleep here?"

"No."

"Are you going to see him again?"

"We didn't talk about it."

She looked skeptical, and I said, "He did say he wasn't going to be around campus much." I told her he was almost done school and that we didn't even exchange phone numbers.

Actually, I had the feeling I wasn't going to see Tyler again any time soon. After evaluation week it would be winter break and Renee and I would be driving down to California together, and that would be another couple weeks right there, so I didn't know.

But it was okay. I said, "I think the sightings will be rare."

And Renee said, "Like Sasquatch."

I laughed, we both did. Maybe that was it, maybe Tyler was like Sasquatch. A really, really good-looking Sasquatch.

* * *

I had my shift at work in the afternoon but I couldn't focus very well. I kept thinking about the night, and I still kept thinking, *I had sex.*

And then I'd think, *Who else here has had sex in the last twenty-four hours?* There were people in line returning all kinds of equipment, and I was like, *Did they?* A guy came in with a box of tools for the repair area, and I thought, *Him?*

It was like this for a few days.

I'd lost my virginity, but I didn't feel like I'd lost anything. I'd gained entrance into the club of the experienced and it was exciting. The scarlet V had been removed from my bodice, but more importantly it didn't seem so impossible now that someone I desired could desire me back.

Pu-raise Gawd fur vittory.

Maybe I could go play with the Wild Things if I wanted.

PART TWO

We left extremely early in the morning. It was still dark when we got to Reed to pick up Alec, and we drove the whole twelve hours to Ukiah, taking turns at the wheel of Renee's little old Datsun, listening to tape after tape on the stereo.

Turning off the highway and going down State Street was the weirdest thing. Renee and Alec had never been to Ukiah, but at that moment it was like I'd never left and right away I was being sucked into a quiet kind of nightmare. Alec was driving and I told him which way to turn here and there, through the empty, lifeless streets, and the few stoplights where at times we were the only visible car. The low, blocky buildings had the same signs they'd had forever. I could have found my way through town with my eyes closed, but it wasn't a comforting familiarity, it was suffocating.

They dropped me off in front of my dad's apartment complex and continued on to Berkeley. After they drove away and the sound of the car faded, all I heard was silence. The back wall of the Payless across the street loomed behind me, big and flat and stuccoed with chunks of orange gravel, and I went into the driveway, between the carports and the buildings, to my dad's door. I knocked and my dad opened up and the hall light turned us yellow, me with my backpack and him with his holey sweater and gray mustache, smiling and saying, "You made it."

My dad is a nice guy, but he was never exactly a cuddly person. We exchanged the usual stiff, awkward hug, and I put my backpack in my old room, which had nothing in it anymore except the old foam mattress. Then I sat on the couch under the Bosch painting, with its million tiny figures, and my dad sat in his creaky desk chair.

He combed his salt and pepper hair to the side with his fingers and said, "So, how's college?" He was eating a banana and I heard his teeth hitting together.

I said, "Crunchy banana?" and he kind of chuckled because I always made fun of him for things like that. We talked about my classes and the drive down and he asked how my job at Media Loan was going, and he showed me a crusty old math book with Einstein-level problems that he was working on for fun. I didn't tell him about Tyler, that was too personal, and after a while, when we ran out of things to say, we watched *Star Trek* on TV.

It was the one where Spock gets attacked by a flying pancake and to cure him they figure out they have to expose him to extremely bright light, but then he comes out of the chamber blind. And just when everyone feels tragic, Spock recovers because of his special Vulcan inner-eyelids. He gets in a couple of insults at Dr.

McCoy, and then they zoom through space and everyone is happy again.

* * *

The next day my mom came to pick me up so I could spend the day out at her house. My dad's apartment had a sliding glass door to a little patio inside a fence with a gate, and my mom always came through there instead of the front door. The noise from the gate and the sliding glass door announced her arrival because she never bothered knocking. She had on a brown corduroy shirt with dog fur on it and her hair was cut shorter than usual, and she had more gray at her temples than I'd seen before.

Hugging my mom was different than hugging my dad but it was awkward in its own way. I just sort of survived it, like getting a shot. She wasn't a terrible person or anything like that, but we had a hard time getting along. I hadn't lived with her since I was twelve and it was for the best, because the distance helped keep the peace.

After we hugged, my mom smiled and said, "How did you get so tall?"

"I'm only tall compared to you," I said, because I was only five-four, but she ignored me and asked my dad how he was keeping.

He said, "Good, how about you?" And they caught up for a few minutes, cordial as usual. It was always funny to me, being in the same room with the two of them, because it was so rare and because they were so different. I didn't have that many memories of them together as a couple because I was only six when they split up, and now it seemed almost laughable that they were ever married. After my dad, my mom had mostly had girlfriends, and now she'd been with her partner, Willow, for about five years. My dad on the other hand was the eternal bachelor, but he seemed pretty content with it.

After that my mom and I went out to her car, and while we were driving to her house on the windy dirt road, the dusty car windows rattling all over the place, she said, "So, are you making friends?"

I said I was. I'd already told her about Renee, so I told her about Calvin and the Media Loan t-shirts. As with my dad, I didn't tell her about Tyler.

"Sounds like you're a lot better at making friends than you used to be." She rolled her eyes. She may have framed it as a compliment but the eye roll was her way of reminding me of what a failure I'd been in the past, which wasn't even actually true.

When I'd started my freshman year of high school I went through a kind of change socially, and I wasn't connecting with the girls I'd hung out with in eighth grade. We'd become interested in different things and I no longer thought their jokes were funny, and if I made a joke no one laughed, so I had a few very lonely months hating school and my whole life. Then I made the mistake of mentioning to my mom how I didn't have any friends and she got the idea that I was bad at making them, and once she got something in her mind it stuck forever. Pretty soon after that I met Amy and a couple of her friends and that changed everything for me, but it never changed my mom's mind.

So, her eye roll might have been the start of a fight if I'd taken the bait and argued with her about my friend history, but I didn't. I put a lock on my jaw and stayed quiet. I stayed quiet for so long that finally my mom shouted, "Hello?" And then I started wondering why I was visiting her at all.

Once we got to the house though, I could tell she was making an effort to be nice. The dogs heard the car and came bounding out, barking and wagging their tails and sniffing all over me, and my mom kept going, "Look who's here!"

Willow was in the garden, cutting their miniature patch of grass with a pair of scissors and she waved them at me. "Hi there, Talia." And then she said to the dogs, "Leave her alone!"

My mom and Willow showed me all the stuff they were working on around the house and garden, a new grape arbor they had built, a lemon tree they were growing in their greenhouse. The dogs settled down and ran off to the corners to chew on bones, and when the cat came down from the loft and started slinking around my legs I knew I'd get through the day.

We had a weird salad with a lot of sprouts in it for lunch, and then I helped my mom and Willow bring in a big pile of firewood from the driveway and stack it under the eaves of the house. You always had to wear gloves for that kind of thing, in case of any black widows lying in wait. Everything might be going along fine and then if you weren't careful, Zap! Kind of like with my mom, but keeping busy was helpful and it was always better not to stay too long.

*　*　*

I spent the next few days visiting Amy and other friends who were home for the holidays which saved me from dying inside, though I still felt like Ukiah didn't have enough air. Plus, the holiday season wasn't exactly my favorite. When I was little we lit Hanukkah candles and had presents and I'd get really excited about it because I was just a dorky kid, but that fell by the wayside after my parents split up.

Recently my mom had started celebrating Christmas, since she and Willow were living together, and I spent the day at their house again. They'd cut a little tree from the woods and I helped them decorate it with strings of madrone berries, and my mom roasted chestnuts on the woodstove. Willow was crocheting a hat and she asked me which colors of yarn I thought looked good together and the cat jumped into my lap and my mom stoked up the fire. Most of the evening I sat there petting the cat, watching the dogs in their heat-induced oblivion, and the truce between me and my mom held, no altercations, it was even kind of cozy, so I survived it fine.

Later in the night, when my mom and I went out to the car so she could take me back to my dad's, I stood for a minute in the driveway looking at the stars. I found Orion the Hunter and both dippers and a few other constellations I recognized. It was rare to see stars in

Olympia, what with the constant cloud cover, and the constellations were like old friends, because I used to see them almost every night at one of the communes when my mom and I had to walk in the dark to the cabin we slept in. I was really interested in astronomy back then. My dad gave me a set of star charts for my birthday one year and once, in high school, he took me and Amy out into the hills to see Halley's Comet with his binoculars. The comet didn't look like much, just a faint smudge of light in the dark sky, but it was cool to think it only came around once every seventy-five years, and we were getting to see it. If I ever saw it again I'd be ninety years old.

* * *

The next day Amy and I took the bus to the city, and by the time we got to her apartment I could breathe again. We got burritos at our favorite place, La Zona Rosa, and sat in her room listening to Booker T. and the MG's and Aretha Franklin and the Talking Heads. She caught me up on her life and showed me a set of paintings she did for her art class, a bunch of naked guys in black and white that she called her "Penis Series," inspired by Joseph, the new guy she was seeing.

We were cutting up magazines to make postcards, and Amy said, "So how do you feel about one-night stands?" I'd told her about Tyler.

I said, "I wouldn't want to make a habit of it." I was gluing a picture I'd cut out--the silhouette of a person sitting under a tree--over a night sky background I'd found. Looking at the stars on Christmas night had reminded me of talking with Hari about peace, and I was making this card for him. I said, "What about you?"

Amy said, "I think a one-night stand is fine if you're actually having fun, but it's not really my thing."

I said, "Seems like Joseph is your thing."

She laughed. "He is."

Amy asked me what I was looking forward to in the new year and I said I was pretty excited about the new dance class I signed up for, this style of classical dance from India called Orissi. I'd seen the professor, Dr. Sundara, perform once in the fall and it blew my mind. The movements were so intricate and striking, I didn't know what I was looking at but I couldn't tear my eyes away, and when I found out you had to have previous dance training to take the class I wrote her a letter about my four years of karate and she agreed to let me try.

Amy said, "You'll be able to do it, I'm sure."

She was taking capoeira classes now and she was already getting good at it. When she showed me a few of the moves she said that her previous yoga obsession had helped her, because of the core strength and flexibility she got from it. She was sitting there practically in the splits, perfectly comfortable, working on her cards. I said, "If only I was as athletic as you."

* * *

On New Year's Eve Amy hosted a party and I met her new boyfriend, who shook my hand in a very friendly way and brought a lot of good music and I could see right away why she liked him so much. A couple of our high school friends came and we danced forever and the party was fun, even if people got a little too smashed. At one point, I visited the bathroom and Amy was in there by herself with the big bucket of paste we'd used for the postcards. She was gluing toilet paper to the walls, and since that was the kind of thing that made me love Amy I immediately started helping her.

I didn't care why she was gluing toilet paper to the walls, art didn't need a reason. I'd graduated from high school, lived in Marin, and then moved up to Olympia and started college. I'd met Renee and Tyler and lost my virginity and come back for a visit to Ukiah and now I was here in San Francisco again, and all those normal facts were just as absurd as this toilet paper debacle in Amy's bathroom. And now we were walking through the door of time into a brand-new year. I slapped a piece of toilet paper onto an exposed pipe and then I grabbed Amy and hugged her around the waist and she laughed. 1990 was looking pretty hopeful.

1

I saw the carpenter from the farm again, one Thursday night after my new dance class.

The Orissi class was difficult right away, even though we were starting with the absolute basics. Along with learning positions and footwork and hand gestures, and how to coordinate body parts and build muscles, we had to memorize vocabulary and learn a lot of concepts. Dr. Sundara called this the grammar of the dance, and you had to learn the grammar before you started learning the language. I felt like a clown half the time but I was pretty thrilled to be learning, and when I looked around it didn't seem like I was doing any worse than anyone else.

So that Thursday after class, after putting out so much energy mentally and physically, I was so hungry I headed straight to The Corner to eat. I didn't think I'd live long enough to cook dinner for myself. The line wasn't too bad, and after I got my food I sat in an arm chair, and just when I was all arranged and about to take a big bite of vegan lasagna I realized I was looking at him, the carpenter. I lowered my fork down. Then I had to stare at it for a minute before I could look up again.

He was a couple of chairs away writing in a notebook, with a little stack of empty dishes by his feet. He was writing with one hand, and leaning his head on his other hand, and suddenly it was like I was on the edge of a diving board. I tried to work out how I might say hello but before I got any further he turned his head and looked right at me. His eyebrows drew together. I could tell he sort of recognized me but probably didn't know from where, and I blurted out, "I saw you at the farm."

He smiled. "Oh, yeah... You had a tape recorder or something, right?"

"I did, yeah." I was quite surprised he remembered.

"School project?"

"Sort of."

He nodded and smiled again, his eyes crinkling at the corners, same as before. I asked him if he worked for the college, and he said just an occasional job, he wasn't a student anymore.

He said, "But I build sailboats, mostly. That's my passion." He was smiling a lot actually.

I said, "Oh, cool."

I was going to ask him about that, but he said, "What do you do? I mean, what are you studying?" And I said I didn't have a focus yet, this was only my first year.

He leaned forward, "First year, huh? Are you from around here?"

"No, I'm from California."

"Oh, yeah? Whereabouts?"

I told him, and he said, "Is that up around Mendocino?" I said it was about an hour inland from

Mendocino, and he goes, "An hour!" like that was remarkable. He shook his head. "I could never live that far inland. I have to be by the water."

I said, "Sailboats and everything?"

"And everything." He bounced a bit in his chair, kind of restless. I was feeling restless myself now, my legs felt twitchy but I was sitting on them so it didn't show.

He stuck his pen behind his ear and closed his notebook. Then he took the pen off his ear, half-laughed, said, "Force of habit," and put it in the pocket of his flannel shirt. He said, "So what classes are you taking?" He really seemed interested, and after I told him, he said, "Okay, so you're like arts and humanities?"

"Right." His smile was pretty contagious.

"I was mostly science. Ecology." He said he liked the field classes best, he liked to be outside in the elements.

I said, "Being a carpenter and building boats must be good for that."

"Oh, it is." He nodded, ran a hand through his dark hair. "I'm George, by the way."

I said, "I'm Talia."

He said, "Nice to meet you."

"You too." My voice completely squeaked.

Then he glanced around to check the clock on the wall behind us. It was almost seven, and he said, "I better get going." He picked up his dishes from the floor. "Maybe I'll see you around." His brown eyes lingered on mine for a second and I felt something, like a little poof of flame in my chest.

I said, "Yeah, see you around." I was slightly overcome, to tell the truth.

After he left I realized I hadn't eaten yet. I'd forgotten about being hungry and now my lasagna was cold, but I really didn't mind.

* * *

The next night I went back to The Corner again. I didn't know if I was more nervous that George the carpenter wouldn't be there or more nervous that he would be, but when I spotted him up near the counter I felt ill. He wasn't just really good-looking, he seemed like a person I wanted to get to know, and I really wished I would calm down a little.

Luckily, he didn't see me at first. He was checking out the menu on the chalkboard, and had obviously been working because his pants were muddy at the knees and coated with sawdust. He wasn't a big guy, but he was broad in the chest and shoulders, and I watched him from the corner of my eye. I wondered if he'd want to talk to me again, because you just never know about people. And then he looked back and saw me and did a bit of a double take between me and the chalkboard.

I felt like such an idiot standing there, but he walked over, and I was just thankful for my backpack because I could hold onto the straps. At that moment if I hadn't had something to do with my hands it would have been the biggest disaster of my life.

He ducked his head down a little and smiled, kind of shy. "Hey, here we are again." He stuck his hands in his pockets. "You want to eat together?"

"Yeah, sure." I barely squeaked it out.

Once we got our food we sat in the same arm chairs, and he said, "What was the name of the town you're from again?"

"Ukiah." My voice was working now.

"Right. You miss it?"

I said, "Not really. I mean I miss some things, but I kind of have a hard time being there." I told him I'd just been there during winter break and even though I'd been away a long time it was still claustrophobic. I said, "I should probably be over that by now."

But he said, "No, I get it. I'm from Bellingham, I feel the same way."

I was kind of amazed we had that in common and I asked him how big Bellingham was. He said about forty-five thousand people, and I said that was three times the size of Ukiah. He said, "You can't help how you feel, though." He said Bellingham was actually bigger than Olympia but having grown up there made it feel smaller. But it all depended. He said his brother still lived up there and usually liked it fine.

I asked him if he had a big family and he said, "Just my mom and my brother, pretty much. My dad's in Oregon, and most of the other relatives are back east." I said that was similar to my situation, except that I didn't have siblings, though I always wished I did, and he said his brother was one of his best friends.

After we finished eating we kept sitting there talking. The more he told me, the more I wanted to know, and I hoped he didn't have anywhere he had to get to. Before long, the food area closed down and people started setting up a PA system for the open-mic they had there

Friday nights. Renee always called it "Men with Guitars Night," since that was most of the line-up.

I asked George how he got into building sailboats and what he loved about it.

He said, "I'll probably bore you if I really get started."

"I doubt it."

He laughed. Then he said that what was really exciting about it was that there were so many elements working together—the properties of the wood, the wind, the water, all the interacting shapes. He smiled. "It's very dynamic."

I tried not to, but for a minute I got fixated on the *interacting shapes* idea, and how deranged it would be if I said, *I'd like to interact with* your *shapes*.

The music was starting up now and it was getting hard to hear. George scooted his chair next to mine and to keep talking we had to lean in, and his face was so much closer and I could feel his body heat and I thought I was going to melt into the chair.

When the men with guitars finally finished, it was about ten. We'd been sitting there almost four hours but it hardly seemed like any time at all. Right then I remembered something and I kind of jumped up.

"Oh, no."

"What?"

I was supposed to cut Renee's hair that night. Nothing critical, but she'd asked me to because her split ends were getting on her nerves. I'd said I would and I didn't want to flake out on her. I said, "I forgot about something I have to do."

George stood up too. "Oh, okay."

Neither of us said anything for a few seconds. Then I said, "Could I give you my number?" It was kind of do or die.

He goes, "Oh, yeah, definitely," and started patting his pockets for his pen. I wrote my number on a blank page in his notebook and then he quickly wrote his name and number on another page and tore it out. He goes, "Here's mine."

I stuffed it in my pocket. I said, "Cool," just as if I did that kind of thing every day.

Then he said, "Hey, I'm going to be over here again on Monday. Would you maybe want to go see my boat?"

"Oh, yeah, for sure. Okay."

"Around three?"

"Three's good."

The next thing I knew I was outside running toward my building. I ran the whole way but I could have run ten times that far.

* * *

When I got home, Renee was in the bathroom trying to cut her hair herself. She had her reading glasses on and a fistful of her hair held up between her face and the mirror, squinting at the ends.

I said, "I'm sorry. I'm sorry I'm so late."

"Phew, you're here." She handed me the scissors. "Where have you been anyway?"

I told her I'd been over at The Corner and gotten into a long conversation. "You weren't doing too bad, actually," I said, trying to focus on her hair.

"What kind of conversation?"

"A really good one." I was smiling my head off, I couldn't help it.

She looked at my face in the mirror. "Sasquatch?"

"Somebody else."

"Name?"

"George." I picked up her towel, scrunched it up to my face and half-laughed, half-screamed into it.

Renee goes, "I've never seen you like this." I shook my head. My face was still in the towel. She laughed. "You are so sprung."

* * *

It rained all weekend. Renee and I spent most of the time on the couches at the apartment, studying. Every time I got up to get tea or a snack or use the bathroom, I'd stare out the window, watching the rain turn the closest edge of the athletic field into a lake and thinking about how much longer it was until Monday at three.

Renee said, "You'd think the sky would run out of water by now."

"Seriously."

She said, "Damn, my highlighter is out of ink."

I said, "Use mine."

* * *

The sky did run out of water though, temporarily, because by Monday afternoon it was halfway clear, and when I went to meet George the walking path was almost dry. He was sitting on the steps going up to The Corner and he stood up when he saw me coming.

He had that shy smile again. "Hey."

"Hey."

"Should we go?"

"For sure."

He goes, "I'm this way." We started walking and he asked how my weekend was and I asked him the same thing. He had a beat-up little pick-up truck with a camper shell made of plywood, and I asked him if he made it, the camper.

"I did, yeah." He opened up the door on the passenger side of the truck and then went around to the driver's side. "It's kind of slap-together job though. I'm working on a better one." It looked good to me and I said so, and he said, "I try."

George had a quick way of driving, spinning the wheel with one hand and working the gear shift with the other and checking the mirrors, all rapid second-nature while keeping up the conversation. I wasn't that great at driving, since I never had a whole lot of practice, so I tended to notice when people were good at it, and pretty soon we were flying down the road.

We drove out to a boatyard where his boat was up on blocks with pieces of wood scattered around on the ground. I could tell it was kind of his baby by the way he ran his hands over the sides. I didn't know anything about sailing and he pointed out various parts of the boat and what he was working on, and like before I just kept wanting to know more, because boats were this big window into his life. Then we walked out onto the pier and sat on the edge, shoulder to shoulder, shapes interacting, and my heart revved up a little. It was still clear out and the sun was already starting to go down and the sky and water glowed with colors.

He said, "Do you know much about the Puget Sound?"

"Nothing, really."

He told me how it was formed by glaciers, how massive sheets of ice spread and retreated in different glacial periods and carved it out. Gradually, as the land and flow of the water changed, the vegetation and the animal life followed, and the seawater coming that far inland gave rise to miles and miles of new coastline, with a new ecology all its own. He moved his hands around, describing the changes.

As we were talking I kept noticing things about George's face, like the olive tone of his skin and the curves of his cheekbones and his nose, and I started thinking how it takes a while to really see what a person's face looks like. I thought how it was kind of like hearing a song, how the first time you hear it might not even make that big an impression on you, but once it becomes familiar the beauty of it starts to come out.

George said there were all kinds of wildlife out there. He said, "You can see orcas in this inlet, in the right season." He pointed out to a place in the distance where the land jutted out into the water. "There's a pass over there they go through."

I said, "I've never seen whales in real life. It must be incredible."

"It is. They're beautiful."

I told him I'd only seen seals, and that when I was a little kid, six or seven, one time I was on a beach and this big wave rose up and there was a seal floating inside the wave, and right before the wave crashed the seal just looked at me, so calmly, like it was looking through a window.

I said, "That was the first time I ever saw a seal, and the whole next day I was so psyched, just because I'd seen it."

George was looking at me. His eyes looked closer. He didn't say anything, but he smiled, and then he reached over and took my hand in both of his. My heart jumped up and started pounding. His hands were warm, and rough from work, and I curled my fingers around his. Heat radiated from his hands and his shoulder and where our hips were touching, and then he leaned in and his lips touched mine.

He didn't have to bend too far because he wasn't a whole lot taller than me, and our teeth hit together a tiny bit but it was okay. I kissed him back, and for a second I got that feeling like I might faint. I had a sudden attack of shyness and I put my forehead on his shoulder. George said, "Do you want to go back to the truck? It's getting pretty cold."

It was pretty cold. I was shaking a tiny bit, but that also might have been from my heart racing. When we were back at the truck again George told me that he'd built the camper shell so he could sleep in the back when the weather was warmer, and he often slept out there, parked at the boat yard, because he liked waking up to the sound of the water. I lifted the hatch and peeked in and it looked like one big bed.

I said, "It looks comfortable."

And he said, "You want to check it out?"

He climbed in first, then sat up on his knees, which made his jeans tight against his thighs, and he held the hatch open for me. When I got in we were facing each other, and we started kissing like mad. He threw the blankets over us and pulled me closer, but we didn't take off any clothes, not even our coats, and he scrunched big handfuls of my hair and put his mouth on my neck. We kept kissing, and I moved on top of him and my head grazed the roof of the camper shell, so I leaned down and he held me and said, "I never want to let you go."

* * *

The next night we met at The Corner again. I knew he was finishing up the job near campus and would be working at another site after that, and when I got there he was standing on the stairs.

I said, "You always beat me."

He laughed. "I'm early once in a while." He had on wool gloves with the fingers cut off but his hands must have been cold because he kind of cupped them over his mouth and blew on them, and then he took my hand. He said, "You want to get something to eat?"

I smiled, "That's what I came for."

"Like in town. My treat. You like Vietnamese?"

"Oh, okay, sure. That would be great."

He let go of my hand and put his in his pockets and kept them there while we walked to where he'd parked his truck.

He said, "Do you get off campus much?"

"Not a lot."

"Neither did I, when I was going here."

I knew he was older, but I didn't know by how much, and when I asked him how old he was he said twenty-six. I said, "Oh," and for a second I panicked, because that sounded extremely old.

He said, "How old are you? Nineteen? Twenty?"

"Eighteen."

He nodded. "Eighteen."

* * *

We sat in a booth on brown seats with cracks in them and ate spicy noodles. The lights were dim and there was a candle burning in a red glass and I asked him what kinds of things he liked besides boats.

"I like some things," he said, crinkling his eyes. Then he said he liked to read and we started talking about books. We both liked Vonnegut and Steinbeck, and I told him how I'd read *The Grapes of Wrath* a few months ago and he said it was one of his favorites.

I said it had a big effect on me, maybe especially because I was traveling at the time, moving up to Olympia.

He said, "Did your parents bring you up here?" I said no, I took the bus, and he said, "That's kind of a big move, by yourself."

I said, "I was already out of school though. For a year." I told him about living in the Bay Area and working at the food co-op.

"I guess your parents aren't too overprotective of you then."

I laughed. "No."

We started talking about books again, and he listed off several of his favorites but I hadn't read them. He said, "Let me loan you a couple books. Do you have time to stop by my house?"

* * *

We drove up to a clapboard house on a side street not far from downtown, a duplex. It was raining again and he pushed the door open with a little effort because the wood was swollen. Inside a man and a woman were cooking in the kitchen.

The man looked up from under a mass of kinky blond-brown hair. "Hey, Jor." The woman smiled, she had almond-shaped eyes and shiny black hair to her waist.

"Marco, Anita," he said, introducing me, and told them I was a student up at the college. "We're going to look at my bookshelf."

I was sure I was blushing but glad it wouldn't show because the light was off in the entryway. They were all, like, grown-ups.

"Okay, Man." Marco was busy cutting vegetables, and Anita smiled again and gave a little wave.

George's room was down the hall. He had a wall full of maps of the Sound and a batiked cloth hanging from nails over the window. There was a futon on the floor and milk crate and board bookshelves like everyone had, and below the maps a big metal desk with all kinds of stickers on the sides, bands and political stuff. He stepped through the door after me, shut it and leaned against it.

The door made a click behind him. Right then I remembered this old Sex-Ed movie from Health class where this guy expected a girl to put out because he had taken her to dinner, and here I was, lured to George's room with the promise of a book, and without even meaning to I said, "I know karate."

He goes, "Really?"

"Yeah."

"Show me something."

I was hardly in top form, it had been so long, and I was never incredible at karate anyway, but I still knew one pretty good move. I told him to make like he was going to stab me with a knife, and when he did I got my arm under his and forced his shoulder down, so he was bent over and half-pinned.

"Shit!" He burst out laughing. His face was red when he stood up. "You were serious." He raised his hands up, "Don't worry, I won't try anything. I'm a lover, not a fighter."

A lover, not a fighter. I bit on my knuckle. That Sex-Ed moment had passed and I was back to reality and the truth was I completely wanted to be there.

I said, "Okay, then maybe you can show *me* something."

"Like some moves?" He boxed at the air a couple of times, then he shook his head. "No, I couldn't do that." He took my hand. His gloves were in his back pocket and I felt his rough palms. He said, "No moves. I just follow my heart."

I thought he was going to kiss me, but he pulled me over to the bookshelf and we sat on the floor. He took down a few books, saying what he liked about them, and

I said I didn't have a lot of time to read for fun because I had so much reading for school, and he said, "How about just this one?" It was Ken Kesey, *One Flew Over the Cuckoo's Nest*. He said, "You can take your time with it. If you want."

I turned it over in my hands. The cover was worn and the design was cool. I'd never read Ken Kesey but I'd heard of him. "Thanks."

He asked if I should be getting back. He said, "It's a school night, right?"

I said, "Pretty soon."

He nodded and smiled and didn't say anything, but kept looking at me, which was kind of embarrassing. I looked down and he put a hand on the knee of my jeans and rubbed my thigh and I put my hand on top of his. He came closer, kissed my cheek and lingered there, waiting to see what I'd do, and I kissed him back, on the mouth, and he brought a hand up to my jaw and stroked the side of my neck.

That same feeling I had when we made out in his truck came flying up from my belly and we kissed harder, and after a minute he asked me if I wanted to go on the bed. He goes, "Maybe you can do more karate on me."

"Okay."

He lay back on the bed and I straddled him, and I felt his erection against my crotch, through our clothes. He gripped my hips, pressing me to him as we kissed, and it was like tongue wrestling at that point and the thought of that made me laugh.

He goes, "What's funny?"

I rolled off him and he turned on his side, raising up to an elbow. His cheeks were red and there was sweat at his hairline.

"Nothing."

"Oh, come on." He rubbed my arm.

"Just... tongue wrestling," I said, and he laughed too.

"The best sport there is," he said. "One of." Then he turned onto his back and groaned and pressed the heels of his hands to his eyes, and he said, "Jesus. Are you really eighteen?"

"Is that a problem?"

"It might be."

"Why?"

And he said, "Don't make me say it." I poked him in the ribs and he crunched up. "Hey, I'm ticklish."

"Tell me." I had this sudden nervous feeling that he'd think I was too much of a child.

"Oh, it's... you know." He rubbed his eyes again. "It's like either we're going to have sex and I'm going to regret it, or we're not, and I'll regret that too."

I was kind of shocked he said that out loud, but it was also exciting, and I thought that this must be the way grown-ups talked.

"Why regret, though?" I asked. Tyler talked about regret, said he didn't want us to do anything I would regret, and I wondered what the deal was with sex and regrets.

And George said, "Because I like you too much already."

"And I'm eighteen?"

"Yeah, and it's your first year here, and there's lots of guys around, and, you know, you aren't likely to want to…"

"Want to what?"

"You know, stick with me." He looked over at me. "I mean, that's cool. I think that's how it's supposed to be."

I looked at him, lying there, with his warm brown eyes and dark brows, and lips all sort of moist from kissing. He had such a sweet expression. I thought how he had to know about a lot of things that I didn't yet.

I said, "I don't know my future."

It seemed like the bare truth. I touched the edge of the pillow and walked two fingers like a pair of legs over to the top of his head, and then gently walked them over his face, touched his lips, and then walked them down to the middle of his chest. He was strong from his work and the outlines of his muscles showed through his shirt, not like a muscle man, just strong, and I laid my hand flat there, feeling his heart beating.

"You said you follow your heart."

He put his hand over mine. "I did say that."

* * *

George drove me home, moving his hand back and forth between the gear shift and my knee, and we were both quiet, listening to the rise and fall of the engine and the spray of rain against the windshield. He pulled the truck up in the round-about near my area of the dorms, took off his seatbelt and laid his arm on the back of the seat, facing me. He touched my ear with his fingertips.

"Thanks for coming out."

"Thanks for the book, and dinner and everything."

He moved forward so we could kiss again. The neck of his t-shirt showed under his flannel, and because it was a bit stretched out part of his collar bone showed on one side. I reached up and touched the place on his neck where his olive skin held a shadow. Then I pulled the cloth down a little and kissed him there, and his exhale came out with a tremor in it.

He got out when I did and came around to give me a long hug, and then he stepped back, accidentally stumbling off the curb, and we both laughed.

George said he'd be at a jobsite across town for the rest of the week, but he said, "Maybe see you on the weekend?"

"I'm around," I said, and waved.

* * *

When I went inside, I found Renee reading in her room with her door open.

I leaned in. "Hi."

"Do you need this back?" She was still using my highlighter and held it up.

"No, it's okay." I stepped inside her door. "Did you have practice today?"

Renee had joined the women's soccer team and I'd seen her muddy cleats outside the front door. She said she did. I said, "How's Dylan?"

She smiled but rolled her eyes. Dylan was the assistant coach who Renee had a crush on. When she'd originally told me that I'd asked her if Alec knew, and she'd said, "No, but he doesn't need to know. Nothing's going to happen."

Now I wondered how old Dylan was. I said, "How old is he anyway?"

Renee said, "Twenty-four maybe? Around that."

I nodded. I guessed twenty-four wasn't so different from twenty-six. The age thing was bit of a mind-blower but I wasn't fixating on it too much. I was in a daze, to tell the truth, and if I closed my eyes I could still feel George's kiss.

Saturday George called and invited me to a party at his house. He said Anita and Marco had friends who played music and they were going to jam and it was going to be low-key. I wondered if I'd know how to act around George's older friends. I'd been to a number of off-campus parties and didn't feel any more awkward than usual, but this would be George's scene and I didn't want to seem too out of place.

Renee said, "Just bring your blanky and your pacifier and you'll be fine."

I laughed. "Shut up."

* * *

About eight o'clock George's beat-up truck rolled into the round-about and stopped in front of the bench where I was waiting and reading the book he'd loaned me.

"Oh wow," he said. "You dressed up."

I owned virtually nothing other than sweatshirts and jeans but Renee had loaned me a dress and a pair of boots, and when I put it all on she told me I looked yummy. The dress was black with white flowers and buttons up the front and a neck opening that dipped down to the top of my bra. I had on the beaded necklaces I always wore, and under the dress, woolen long johns. I'd seen George in his work clothes, heavily spattered in paint and saw dust, and the clothes he was wearing now looked about the same except clean, but he looked nice. His hair was wet like he'd just taken a shower and he'd shaved, and somehow his eyelashes were more noticeable now that he'd shaved, thick and black.

* * *

The party at George's house wasn't the loud and crowded kind, it was low-key like he'd said. Drinks were piled up on the kitchen counters and people were sitting around the living room with guitars and drums and other instruments, and there were candles burning everywhere. The music was folksy and mellow. I really liked it, but it was hard to talk over. George sat in an arm chair and I sat next to him on the end of a sofa and tucked my feet up under me, and he took a drink of his beer and then reached over to stroke my pinky finger. It was our first touch of the night and it brought heat to my cheeks.

I wasn't drinking anything yet. George had asked me what I wanted to drink when we got there but I'd said I'd have something in a bit. I had a hard time swallowing if I was anxious at all, liquids would go down the wrong way and then I'd cough my head off.

A girl with wavy light brown hair came by and said hi to George. She was wearing tight, faded jeans with a lot of patches and a white blouse that showed some cleavage. Her boobs were pretty big, and she flipped her hair over her shoulder and perched on the arm of George's chair with her back toward me.

He said, "Hey, Kayla."

"Your hair has grown out," she said, touching the back of it.

"Hey, um, meet my friend." He still had a hold of my pinky finger, and she looked over her shoulder at me and gave a little pursed-lipped smile. I flashed her the Vulcan symbol. I hoped it might annoy her but she didn't leave. She was getting on my nerves, to tell the truth.

George stood up, maneuvered around Kayla, and leaned over me. "You want that drink now?"

"Sure."

He took my hand and I followed him into the kitchen.

He goes, "Sorry about that."

I looked into the living room and noticed that Kayla had taken my spot on the sofa.

"That's okay," I said. "Is she a good friend of yours?"

"We went out for a little while," he said. "Last year."

"You've probably had a lot of girlfriends," I said.

"A few."

We looked over the drinks and George asked me what kind of beer I liked and I said I didn't like beer.

"You don't like beer?" He was surprised.

"Ginger beer is pretty good." I'd spotted a six-pack of that on the table and he reached over and handed me one.

I noticed they had those poetry magnets on the fridge and I inspected the words, deciding I'd write George a secret message: *You and me, Trod leaves, Sing to intestines, meaning forest fishing rod.* It made no sense, but it didn't have to because the vibes were strong, at least I thought so. George was standing next to me and kissed the side of my head, on my hair. I wanted to kiss him back, but not while there were other people around.

I hooked my finger into the pocket on his shirt instead. "I'm really liking the book you loaned me."

"Cool," he said. "I'm glad."

He took my hand again and we returned to the living room and this time sat on the floor on pillows a bit way from the music. Marco was on guitar and Anita was singing and she had a good voice, high, a soprano maybe, and she had her eyes closed, swaying from the waist up. Another guy was playing a harmonica and a girl in overalls had a set of bongo drums. It reminded me a lot of my commune days, actually, except for now I was supposed to be one of the adults, rather than one of the kids who ran around playing hide and seek and accidentally got into the pot brownies.

I leaned toward George's ear. "What were you like when you were eighteen?"

"Me?" He ran a hand back through his hair and shook his head. "Oh, man, I was really hyper." He said he rode his bike constantly, because he had to keep moving, and that was when he got into sailing.

"Did you skateboard too?"

"All the time."

"I can picture it."

"Yeah, I used to go down to the Western Washington campus with my friends and skate over everything, benches, stairs..." He shook his head again. "You're a lot more mature than I was," he said. "I was a little nuts."

* * *

By midnight half the guests had left and the rest were talking about going to another party across town where there was supposed to be dancing. George asked me what I felt like doing because he knew I liked to dance, but I said I'd rather stay there, and soon enough everyone cleared out.

Kayla kicked George's foot on her way to the door, "Have fun tonight."

He goes, "You too."

Then he gave me a sideways look. "You want to hang out in my room?"

"Sure."

He pulled me up to my feet and we tiptoed down the hall holding hands. He pushed the door open with his shoulder and lit a candle on the bookshelf. Then he closed the door and straddled the chair at his desk backwards, with his arms folded on the back of it. I sat down on the bed. There was a small, carved wooden box on the shelf by the candle and I lifted the lid without asking. It smelled like amber and there were a bunch of condoms inside. Trojans. George was resting his forehead on his arms and I didn't see his face.

I said, "Are you tired?" I was about to be so disappointed if he was.

But he put his chin on his wrist and wagged his head. "Not at all."

"You're far away."

"Ah!" There was a touch of frustration in his voice and he leaned back. "I'm trying not to come on too strong," he said. "I've been told I can be overwhelming."

"Oh." I made a sad face.

Suddenly, in a flash, George jumped up and leap-frogged the chair, tumbling onto the bed next to me, and the startle of it made me scream a little and then we were both laughing. He hovered over me, his dark brown eyes and girl's lashes and his olive skin glowing in the candle light.

He said, "You're so beautiful."

His mouth tasted like beer, and I thought that maybe it was possible to like it after all, and I pulled him down on top of me and wrapped my legs around his, because I'd been waiting all night to kiss him. I'd been waiting for days.

He was hard again, I could feel him, but this time it was different, because maybe we were going to take our clothes off. I touched the buttons of his shirt while we kissed and undid them one by one, and after the last one I pushed the flannel off his shoulders. I lifted up the front of his t-shirt and he grabbed it from the back and pulled it off and I saw the curves of his bare shoulders and the hair on his chest, sort of diamond-shaped, and I put my hand there. He slid his hands up my sides and over the front of my dress and started undoing the buttons, and we took turns like that, still kissing, with the rain beating at the window.

And then we were naked under the covers and I asked him if he was thinking about regret now, and he said, "No, are you?" I shook my head.

He said, "I don't mean to harp on your age, but have you done this before?"

"Had sex?"

"Yeah."

"Once."

"A long time ago?"

"Couple weeks." Actually, Tyler had been more than a couple weeks before, but my mind was not going very linear.

"Do you want to now?"

I nodded. Every part of me was vibrating. I reached for him, bit on his shoulder while he turned back the blanket and got a condom from the box on the shelf. He must have ripped the wrapper too hard, because the condom flew onto the floor, and he half-laughed, "Whoops." But he got another one, and when it was on he moved between my legs and we kissed again and then he found the right place and pushed inside.

It didn't hurt this time, like it did with Tyler, and I didn't feel so clumsy. It was more like being hungry. George was moving out and pushing in and our hips rocked together and I squeezed my legs around him and he moaned. Then he put two fingers in his mouth and reached down to stroke me while we were doing it, with his whole body against me, his mouth on mine, on my neck. I kissed his throat because I loved his voice, coming out here and there in soft, secret noises I wouldn't otherwise have heard. He smelled like sweat and saltwater, amber and beer, and flowery traces of shampoo, and between my legs the sensations built up and up until I thought I was going to--I didn't know what--die maybe.

And then I was lighting up on the inside, in flashes spreading out into my legs and arms and I squeezed

George's neck so hard I thought I might strangle him, and he moaned into the pillow and crushed me to him, and it was like in that movie where the waves break over the man and woman who are kissing on the beach, but so much better.

We stayed like that until our breathing slowed down. The candle was just a nub but it kept burning, and George moved away to get rid of the condom. I hugged him from behind, and we lay there just breathing.

After a little while, he said, "Should I know about him?"

"Who?"

"The guy from a couple weeks ago."

"Oh, him. Tyler."

Long pause. "Are you seeing him too?"

"Just that one time."

Longer pause. "You like him?"

I considered this. Maybe I liked Tyler. It had been a while and I hadn't been thinking about him much. I did like him, before, but I never liked him the way I liked George.

"I like you," I said, which was the bare truth.

My hand was resting on his belly and he moved it up to his chest and held it there. Under the flesh and bone and damp wisps of hair I could feel his beating heart, and my own heart pressed up against his back, and I wondered about liking and I wondered about love.

After that George and I started seeing a lot of each other. When we stayed the night together it was mostly at his house, and occasionally he stayed over with me but he said he didn't want to infringe. On weekends I'd on his bed with my back against the wall, reading for class, and he'd sit at his desk with his drafting tools, drawing on big pieces of graph paper designs for sailboats he wanted to build one day. We took walks and ate, and often, though he offered to drive me home, I took the bus, because I needed a stretch of quiet. Being so close to another person was sometimes dizzying.

Instead of the old empty ache, I was feeling something else, fed and nourished and brilliant, like every day was my favorite song. It was amazing to me that I could touch George whenever I wanted and that he liked it. Even aside from the sex part, I'd never been so tactile with anyone and it was like it made life go from black-and-white to Technicolor. Once in a while though I also had this feeling of being exposed, as if I'd walked out of the house in my underwear and all my usual perimeters were in flux. I'd be on the bus going home and I'd zip up my coat even if I wasn't cold and say to myself, *I'm still me. I'm just me.*

* * *

One morning when I was at George's and I was reading and he was at his desk, I got up to have a look at what he was drawing and I sat on his lap. He tossed his pencil onto the desktop and put his hand on my back.

He goes, "You're going to break my concentration," but I could hear him smiling, and while I was looking at the drawing I shifted so I was pressed against his crotch. I was only wearing a sweatshirt and a pair of boxer shorts and I felt him getting hard.

We started kissing, and the fire roared up between us and I said, "Don't move," and I climbed off him and grabbed a condom from the box on the shelf.

His cheeks were flushed, and he goes, "What are you doing?"

And I said again, "Don't move."

My fingers were shaking, but I undid his fly and he was very hard, and I tore the condom open and put it on him myself, and then I slipped off my boxers and straddled him. He slid inside me and moaned. I wrapped my arms tight around his neck and we moved together and the chair creaked. Then all of a sudden he grabbed me with all his strength and lifted me up and I gripped him with my legs, and then we were on the carpet, going fast and furious right there on the floor. He came right away, but before I could be disappointed he moved down and kissed my belly, and he went lower and put his mouth right on me. I felt his tongue moving around with all that fire and I pressed myself against him until it was all over for me.

When I could think again, I thought, *Jesus, this sex thing is crazy.*

Other times we'd be reading or watching a movie and I'd start to get interested in George instead, and certain body parts like his neck or the back of his ear would become like magnets to me. Or in bed I'd get fascinated by the line of black hair than ran from his belly button down to his crotch or the dip of his spine when he lay on his stomach, and I'd have to kiss them and lick them like an animal. It was pretty thrilling because George loved it, and he had his own wildness and we just kept playing this wild game.

* * *

One Saturday night we walked down to a bar with Marco and Anita to shoot some pool, and when I said I hadn't ever played much pool Marco said he'd give me some pointers. Anita liked to tease him and she said, "He thinks he's an expert."

Marco brought the cue he was holding to his lips and goes, "Shhh," at her.

George went to the bar to get a beer for himself and a ginger beer for me, and as Marco was setting up the balls in a triangle who should I see but Handsome Sasquatch. Tyler.

He glanced over from where he was talking with a group of people at a table and then he got up and came over. He smiled, "Hey, is that Talia?" I'd sort of forgotten how tall he was.

It was nice to see him, but it was pretty awkward, especially when George came back. George looked at Tyler and looked at me, and kind of sized things up. He gave me my ginger beer and then put his arm around me, and I could tell he was letting Tyler know what the deal was. Tyler took the hint and he said, "Well, I just wanted to say hi," and he smiled again, and as he was walking away he turned around and said, "Maybe I'll see you on the dance floor," and that made me blush, because it was right in front of George, and it was all pretty confusing.

George was kind of jumpy after that. We played pool and Marco did give me his helpful hints and George was maybe quieter than usual. Then when Tyler and his friends left, and he and I just waved very casually, George seemed more relaxed.

Once we were back at his place it seemed like he had something on his mind and I figured it had to do with seeing Tyler. We were lying on his bed with a candle burning on the shelf. George was looking up at the ceiling and he said, "I know we haven't made things exclusive, and I don't know how you feel, but I don't want us to see other people. I mean, I don't want us to see other people while we're seeing each other."

It seemed like it was a little hard for him to get this out, which surprised me because I just assumed we weren't seeing other people, so I said, "I already thought we weren't seeing other people." And then I got a bit nervous and said, "Have you seen anyone else? I mean, since we got together?"

Suddenly I felt like it would be terrible if he had, but he turned toward me and said, "No. No, of course not."

I think we were both kind of relieved. I touched his hair and put my hand on his cheek. Every day George was bigger to me. I was becoming his and he was becoming mine, and this pulled something out of me. My guts were getting tangled up with his guts, and it was terrifying, but it was also the best thing that had ever happened. I put my arms around him and he kissed my forehead, and our shadows flickered on the wall when a draft blew at the candle flame.

* * *

In the morning while George was in the shower, Anita offered me a cup of tea in the kitchen. I said, "Sure, thanks," thinking how if I was into girls I would probably be in love with her, because she was super cool and so beautiful. While we were drinking the tea, I asked her what her heritage was. I'd wanted to ask her that before but was kind of shy about it.

She took a sip from her cup and said, "Japanese-American and European-American."

I'd been reading a book for class on the World War Two internments and I asked if those affected her family.

She nodded. "Yeah, my dad's parents were farmers and they lost everything."

"That's so awful."

She said her dad's earliest memories were from the camp they were forced into, and that it really affected him and that when she and her sisters were growing up he always told them that they needed professions that were portable. That had a lot to do with why she became a teacher.

I said, "Actually that reminds me of stories my dad used to tell about his parents. The whole community was kicked out of their town in Poland, and being educated and portable was the important thing."

Anita goes, "That's right." She taught social studies in middle school and she said that the other reason she became a teacher was because it was so important for kids to learn about that stuff. She said, "My goal is to turn my students into little revolutionaries."

I laughed. "You must be a great teacher."

I'd asked George about his heritage when we'd first started hanging out and he'd said it was mostly Portuguese and English, and that he didn't know a whole lot about it but his Portuguese grandfather was a fisherman out in Maine and the ocean was kind of in his blood. Anita finished her tea and I was just finishing mine when George came in the kitchen. He was still steaming from the shower and he didn't have a shirt on and just like that I forgot all about the importance of history.

* * *

That afternoon we went sailing in a sailboat that George sometimes borrowed from a friend, since his own boat was under permanent construction. We'd go out for just an hour or two at a time, when the weather was good and it was beautiful out on the water, but the thing I liked most about sailing with George was seeing George sailing. He was relaxed in a way I didn't normally see him, but his movements were quick and alert, pulling the ropes and ducking under the boom, all second nature, like the way he drove his truck, but more so. He said when his boat was finished we should go out to the San Juan islands, maybe in the summer, and even though water wasn't my element the way it was his I thought it would be pretty incredible to go.

When George took me home we hung out in my room a while. He sat on the bed and while I was folding laundry he started fiddling around with some embroidery thread I'd had lying on my desk. We were talking and I wasn't really paying attention to what he was doing, and when I was finished I sat next to him.

"What are you making?"

He was turning the embroidery thread into a kind of knotted cord. "These are my favorite sailing knots." He said you couldn't see them properly because the thread was too miniature, but to me the different colors made each knot look like a tiny work of art. I watched him and he told me the names of the knots, and when he was finished he laid it over my palm and smiled. "Here."

I said, "I think you made me a necklace."

"I think I did."

I took off my beaded necklaces and tied George's cord around my neck instead. "I love it." I really did. Actually, I had wanted something from him I could keep close to me. Sometimes I worried it was all a dream. "Thank you." I kissed him on the lips.

He said, "Can you thank me again?"

I said, "I might get creative."

"Oh, please do."

* * *

George called up one night. "Do you have time to go out for a bit? I promise not to get you home too late." He sounded excited.

I said, "What for?"

He goes, "I want to show you something."

We drove out to a house on one of the inlets and parked at the end of a dark, gravel driveway. For once the sky was mostly clear and there was a half moon, like a bright chipped tooth, and a lot of stars out. Orion was high up, faded because of the moon, but his belt was clear, and it pointed down toward Sirius, the dog star, following him.

I held George's arm and he said, "This way," and we stumbled along in the dark down this rocky path to a little dock.

There was just enough light to see the shape of a rowboat there, making a soft thud every time it hit against the dock and tiny waves that splashed back on themselves. George climbed in first and then held onto the dock to steady the boat while I got in. He groped around to untie the rope and get the oars up into the locks and I helped him push off.

He goes, "Look in the water."

"Where?"

"Right here, watch where the oars go in."

All of a sudden, I was looking at something bright and blue. The water was sparkling. Every time the oars dipped in thousands of tiny blue lights lit up, making swirling clouds. "What *is* that?" I kind of screeched and George burst out laughing.

"It's phosphorescence. It's a special kind of plankton that absorbs the sun's energy and emits it in the water. Motion sets it off."

"I've never seen this."

"No, it's seasonal."

I leaned over the side and put my hand in the water, more blue lights. They flashed up with every movement and then slowly died away. I couldn't believe it. I said, "Is this real?"

George laughed again. "Yeah."

We were out a ways now, and he pulled up the oars and put them back in the bottom of the boat and moved closer to me. I cupped some water in my hand and tossed it in the air to see if it glowed, and it didn't really, unless you counted its faint catch of the moonlight and the splash when it fell back down. And while I was still entranced, leaning over the side of the boat, George started rubbing my leg, from the ankle up to my hip bone and down again, and I swear I felt just like the phosphorescence when he touched me.

His fingers trailed over my knee and he said, "I love you, Talia," and he leaned forward and kissed me gently on the mouth, and it was like the sparkling blue lights too, and the stars and moonlight and everything gentle and luminous. The boat rocked in the small waves and I moved so that my lips brushed his ear and I whispered into the curves of it that I loved him too.

I loved him too.

George came by one day to drop off one of my notebooks that I accidentally left at his house, and he stayed just a few minutes because it was the middle of his workday. Renee was getting her things together to go to her shift at the photo lab and she was in a massive hurry and she came around the corner and, Boom! collided with George. And even though it wasn't anyone's fault, he goes, "Whoa, Renee, sorry about that!" because George was pretty unassuming. Later on, when Renee and I were eating dinner, she looked at me and she said, "I like your boyfriend."

That really made me smile. "Cool."

"Yeah, he seems like a really good person. He's very respectful."

"So nice of you to say."

I'd already told her a long time ago how much I liked Alec. He wasn't visiting quite as much lately though. Renee had been hanging out socially with the soccer crowd, including Dylan, the assistant coach, and Alec was having a hard time with it. Renee had said that nothing had changed between them, but there was a strain.

***

A couple of weeks before the spring break, on a Sunday morning when George was at my place and we were making breakfast tacos with Renee, he said, "Hey, Talia was telling me about your photography. Anything you'd feel like showing?"

She smiled. "I could do that."

After we ate she brought out a box of her photos, a lot of big black and white prints she'd made. Some were from this year and others from before, mostly informal portraits—her aunt playing guitar, her three cousins clowning around on a front porch, her grandparents, quite a few of Alec. We spread them out on the table.

"Wow, these are really good, the way you captured the light and their expressions," George said. "How'd you get into it? School?"

Renee said her grandfather was a photographer, she had one of his old cameras, and seeing his photographs growing up was how she got interested. "He was the family documenter," she said. "Maybe I wanted to pick up where he left off."

I'd seen Renee's photos before, but it was fun to look at them again, I thought they were really inspiring, and George kept asking her questions about light and exposure and contrast, and I could see she appreciated the fact that he liked her work so much. I started to get this warm feeling watching them, these two people who had in a short time become so important to me sort of connect with each other.

Then after Renee put the photos away she got out her camera and she said, "Let me take a few of you guys."

*　*　*

A few days later Renee had an errand downtown and she gave me a ride to George's. We all hung out for a while listening to a ska record that George had on the stereo in the living room, because he was heavily into ska, and George goes, "So you guys both lived in Berkeley, huh?"

I said, "Yeah, but we know it in different ways, since I was so young. To me it's kind of like a dreamland."

And Renee goes, "And I didn't have to escape it so badly like she did Ukiah."

George was pacing around, throwing a bottle cap in the air and catching it, because he could never sit still for very long. He said, "You probably wanted to leave though, right? New horizons?"

"Totally."

"And here you both are in Oly-Wa."

Renee goes, "Yep, here we are."

Right then, without warning, George took this big leap and he jumped over the coffee table and landed on the couch next to me. And he goes, "My lucky day!" and he kissed me on the mouth right in front of Renee and she shrieked and laughed and it took me a second to catch my breath.

George laughed too, because he caught me so by surprise, and Renee goes, "I think Talia's pretty happy about it."

* * *

Calvin and I still had a long shift together at work on Fridays and one afternoon when things were relatively quiet and we were sorting adaptors into their different bins, he said, "So, how's it going with George?"

I said, "Pretty great."

He laughed. "Can you not smile when you talk about him?"

"I guess not."

I asked him how it was going with Tristan, this guy he had recently started seeing, and Calvin said he definitely liked him but wasn't sure they were entirely compatible. He said, "Tristan is really into chess, so I don't know."

I laughed, "What's wrong with chess?"

"Just not my thing."

We kept sorting a while, then Calvin said, "Has George been tested yet?"

He meant for HIV. Calvin was active in the ACT UP group on campus and took the issue more seriously than most people did. Two friends of his from Seattle had died of AIDS and he knew how many thousands of people were expected to die of it that year in the US. Actually, it was equal to the entire city of Bellingham.

I said not yet, but I'd been meaning to talk to him about it. I said, "We're being safe."

Calvin said, "Talia, don't put it off."

I took it seriously too though, Calvin didn't have to worry about me. All through high school I'd watched news reports on the new deadly disease with no known treatment or cure, and how fast it was spreading, and how your only hope was to prevent it. Once I told Renee that before, when all I did for sex was entertain myself, anytime I pictured doing it I put a condom in the scenario because I wanted to train my mind, and she'd said she didn't know whether to laugh or be impressed.

Calvin pulled apart a long string of adaptors and cables and started tossing the parts into the right bins, kind of frowning. He said, "You know you can't suck his dick unprotected, right?"

I felt my eyes bulge out. "I know."

Calvin picked up two quarter-inch adaptors and tapped the male ends together. "It's not all male-to-male transmission."

"Oh, my God."

We both laughed. Then he started going off on the male-to-female straight adaptors, and the male-to-male and female-to-female gay ones. And I said I guessed the Y adaptors were bi, and Calvin said, "Damn, this place is sexy."

* * *

Late on another Friday a few weeks later, George picked me up to go stay at his place. The night was cold and windy and wet, and when we got to his house he turned off the engine and said, "So... I got that test."

My stomach dropped through the floor.

"Already?"

He said, "I didn't want to wait, but I didn't want you to worry, so I didn't mention it until I got the results." And then he said that he was negative and it had been over six months since he was with anyone else and everything checked out, and I practically fainted right then and there.

I put my arms around him. "Phew..." He rubbed my elbow and said he hadn't been too worried, but you never know, because he hadn't always made good decisions in the past. And when I'd recovered I thought how this opened up some options for us, namely because I hadn't wanted to put a condom in my mouth. The street was dark and there wasn't a soul around and George and I kissed, and I reached down and squeezed the crotch of his pants.

He goes, "Are we celebrating?"

"I think we should."

He touched my neck. "That's exciting."

I started undoing his fly. I could feel him getting hard, and I put my fingers around it and bent down. He was so hard now, but the skin was silky smooth, and I moved my lips around to feel the shapes of it and tasted him with my tongue. He ran his fingers in my hair and was breathing harder and he kind of whispered, "Oh, God," a few times, and I sucked on him and felt myself getting wet. Then he pushed a bit on my shoulder, and I backed up and he came and caught it in his hand.

He dropped his head back against the seat and closed his eyes. "Holy shit..."

After a little while he asked me if I'd done that before, with someone else, and I said no, and he said maybe it sounded weird to say but for him it was kind of an honor. I laughed and told him to shut up, but he goes, "No, I mean it." He goes, "I mean it. Your touch is beautiful."

* * *

The next day, when we were walking to his house from the Food Co-op, I asked him how old he was when he lost his virginity. He laughed and said he never knew what I was going to come out with, and I said, "So, how old were you?"

And he goes, "Sixteen."

So, ten years ago. And I thought how ten years ago I was just a kid. I was running around with the other kids at the commune in the hills outside Ukiah, imitating the chickens like we did and butting heads with the goats, and meanwhile George was already a teenager and doing teenage things.

"Who was it with?"

"Oh, my girlfriend at the time."

"What was her name?"

"Ellen."

"Where did you do it?"

And he goes, "Do you really want to be talking about this?" And even though it was slightly excruciating, I said yes, and he said it was at a friend's house.

"How was it?"

"Quick."

"Was it her first time too?"

"I think so."

All of a sudden I had so many questions they were going off like popcorn. I asked him how he felt afterward and what he thought about it, and he said he wasn't sure, he didn't completely remember, but he did remember being pretty psyched. Then I asked him if he did it for himself a lot growing up, like touch himself a lot, and he laughed and shrugged and he said, "Why are you asking me all this?"

I didn't really know, it seemed kind of crazy to me too, to be asking about it, but I was just really interested. Except for Calvin I'd never talked to any other guy about sex, and I also had this feeling that I'd missed out on George's life up until now. He'd had this whole past I wasn't part of and it was like I missed him, so I asked him again and he said, "Yeah, a lot. Everyone does it a lot, you know? At least, especially guys do." I asked him if he did it now, like these days, because it seemed like we were together so often, and he said, "Yeah, sometimes."

I asked him what he thought about when he did it and he said he thought about me.

"You don't have to say that."

And he said it was the truth, though. He said, "I think about you all the time."

"Shut up."

"I can't help it."

And then he dropped the grocery bag and tackled me right onto someone's lawn and I laughed and I said, "Hey, I know karate!"

"Well I know love-karate!"

And he kissed me, and I could have escaped but I didn't want to.

* * *

George's brother, Paulo, came down from Bellingham one weekend for a visit. He was younger than George by two years and was into sailing too but worked as a bike mechanic. I was kind of nervous to meet him because George had told me so much about him and I knew they were so close.

George invited me to meet them after they went mountain biking, and when I got to George's house they were in the front, hosing mud off their bikes. It turned out Paulo looked a lot like George, same hair and coloring but leaner and taller, and his eyes and the shape of his face were a bit different. George had told me before that he took after their dad more, and Paulo looked more like their mom. We didn't shake hands or anything when George introduced us because they were covered in mud like their bikes, but Paulo had this big smile and he waved hi and said, "So you're the girl who likes my crazy brother."

I laughed. "I like him a lot."

He said, "Then you must be crazy too," but he didn't even say it to me, it was meant for George, and George turned the hose on him and they started wrestling for it and laughing, and I just got way out of the way.

After they cleaned up we walked downtown to a pub for dinner and hung out talking in a booth. I asked Paulo what George was like as a brother and he smiled at George and said, "He's a good brother." I asked what he was like when they were growing up, and Paulo said, "Very sadistic."

And George goes, "Hey!"

But Paulo said, "You know how big brothers are. Do you have any?"

I said, "No, I don't have any siblings, but I've seen a few in action."

Paulo looked at George, and he said, "There was the time you vacuumed my hamster."

And George goes, "Jesus, don't tell her that!"

I said, "What? What happened?"

George tried to grab Paulo across the table to make him stop talking, but Paulo ducked, and he said that he had this hamster when they were kids and it got out of the cage and ran away, and then it was gone for three weeks. And then their mom noticed that there was all this insulation coming out of the ceiling and falling into the top shelves of their pantry, which was under Paulo and George's bedroom, and she made George clean it, and he started shoving the vacuum hose up there without really looking, because it was so high up he couldn't really see.

George said, "Talia, it was an accident. And anyway, it had to have already been dead. I mean, it had to have been dead, it was three weeks."

And Paulo goes, "And then our mom had to dig it out of the vacuum bag and I bawled my head off, and I wouldn't let George come to the funeral."

By then I was laughing so hard I was almost peeing in my pants and I clung on to George's arm so I didn't fall off the seat, but I half fell off anyway, and then I had to climb back up with George's help.

Then I tried to catch my breath, and I just said, "Oh, my God."

After that we talked about other things they used to do as kids and what I was studying in school and Paulo's work, and he asked about what it was like growing up in communes, and then we got on to music and the time just rolled along.

Paulo said to George, "Your girlfriend is cool."

And George said, "You can't have her."

Paulo goes, "What is this, the Middle Ages?"

That made me laugh again, but not so maniacally, and then I looked at the big clock over the bar and said maybe I should get going, because the last bus was at eleven, and George said, "Aren't you staying?"

I said, "I mean, I don't want to get in the way of the male bonding."

But Paulo said, "No, Talia, stay. It's not like I'm going to be sleeping in the bed with him. I always sleep on the couch."

George looked at me with his eyebrows raised and I said I'd stay and Paulo said he'd make omelets in the morning and George said Paulo did make really good omelets.

11

During the spring break, George and I drove up to Port Townsend with Marco and Anita to see a ska band. Marco had a little wagon of a car and George and I sat in the back with our back packs stuffed down by our feet. Rolled up in the bottom of mine was a new dress I'd bought for the show.

I'd asked Renee to help me look for a dress because I thought I'd need fashion advice, and we went to some thrift stores and finally found this red dress with a pattern of little purple triangles and an old-timey collar. It was pretty form-fitting on me and on the short side and Renee goes, "This one is really sexy."

I said, "Too much?"

She said, "I don't think so. It's nice to see you in clothes like this."

Orissi class had gotten me more used to clothes that showed my shape, and I wanted something special for Port Townsend because it was the first time George and I were going out of town together. The dress was a little out there for me but I liked it and I said, "I'm taking it."

* * *

We got up to Port Townsend in the afternoon and checked into this motel near the water called the Sea Breeze that looked like it was built in the fifties. George signed for the key and we took our stuff to the room, which was on a different side of the motel from Marco and Anita's room, and we planned to meet up in a while to walk around town and get dinner before the show.

The room was tiny, just enough space for the bed and a night table squeezed in between the bed and the wall, with a lamp and a clock on it and two water glasses, and there was a bathroom with a shower stall. The bed was covered in a blue spread with little tassels all over it and I lay down on my stomach. It was nice to spread out after being crunched up in the car and I said, "Ooh, I like the bed."

George tossed the key onto the night table and sat down next to me. There was a blind over the window made of thin bamboo slats, and the daylight filtered in through the cracks. George put his hand on my back and rubbed it in slow circles.

I closed my eyes. "That feels good."

He rubbed lower on my back and then moved his hand over the butt of my jeans, and he made these slow circles on one butt cheek and then on the other, and then down one thigh and then the other and then slipped his hand between my legs, and I was so wet by then I thought he was going to feel it through the denim.

I said, "How much time do we have?"

He leaned over me to look at the clock and I turned over and he said, "About forty minutes," and I practically tore his clothes off.

And then his arms were around me and his mouth was on mine and he was moving inside me and we rolled around on top of all those little blue tassels. I covered his mouth with my hand and held my breath so we wouldn't make such a racket, and he kind of bit my hand, and then we lay there shuddering until finally we were still.

I said, "You did some serious love-karate on me."

And he said, "Yeah, I'm going to have to remember that."

I looked at the clock and we had ten minutes to get dressed and go, so we hurried up and I got the dress out of my bag. It was kind of wrinkled but I put it on while George was in the bathroom, and when he came out he said, "Where did that come from?" I told him Renee helped me find it and he goes, "You're blowing my mind."

* * *

At dinner I asked them if people danced at ska shows, because I'd never been to one, and Marco goes, "Dancing at ska shows is mandatory."

I said, "Really?"

Anita said to George, "Haven't you told her anything?"

And he said, "Actually, I didn't get around to it. No."

It turned out people seriously danced, and not just any old free-form dancing. There were all these particular moves with a lot of little kicks and it was the coolest thing I'd ever seen. The club was small and the band was hot and people were crammed wall to wall, but there was enough room to dance. George started to show me a few of the moves and I started to get the hang of it and it was exciting as hell to see George dancing like that, because aside from a move here and there, wherever, I'd never really seen him dance.

There were two bands and we danced for hours, and at one point I left the dance floor to get a glass of water from the tank they had set up at one end of the bar, and when I went back to find George he was dancing with this other girl. He was smiling, and she was really shaking her butt around, and I thought, *Does he know her?* And suddenly I was sort of appalled and fascinated at the same time, and I stopped where I was and watched for a minute without him seeing me.

They were dancing away, and she was getting closer to him and kind of jutting her boobs out toward him and then I thought that it had gone too far. I'm not competitive, or at least I never thought I was, but I wasn't going to let some girl get over on my boyfriend, and I was surprised at how much I thought I'd like to go over and seriously push her out of the way. I mean, I'm non-violent and I would never do that, but I was feeling animalistic and I squeezed right between them.

I grabbed George's hand and I said in his ear, "Do you know her?"

"No, no, I was just being friendly."

I didn't even turn around to tell her excuse me or anything, I just took over my spot, and I thought that if anyone was going to shake their butt around right there it was going to be me.

George put his hands on my waist and I could tell he was being honest, that he was just being friendly, and my claws started to retract, and then he was kissing me and kissing me, and then he said in my ear, "You're so fucking sexy."

And I said, "You are."

***

Back at the Sea Breeze, between later that night and the next day at noon when we had to hit the road, George and I got our money's worth out of the bed. And I was so caught up in the rush of it--of all our time together-- the heat, the momentum, that I never expected a fall.

12

One night at the beginning of April I stayed over at George's house and in the morning, when we were still in bed, he said he had something to tell me.

He looked pained and my stomach did a flip even though I had no idea what he was going to say. He told me a friend of his had just offered him a job as crew on a sailing trip to Mexico, a last-minute replacement position, and he said it was a real opportunity for him, kind of an extraordinary opportunity, and that he was seriously considering it.

I reached for his hand because I could already tell he'd be going, and I said, "How long is it for?"

And he said, "Four months."

I breathed out. I'd been holding it. I said, "That's a long time."

"Yeah, it is."

"When would you go?"

"In a week."

That felt like a blow. It was so soon. I hugged him and he started to kiss my face and my eyes got wet and he kissed them. He whispered that he was sorry and that it came totally out of the blue, he never expected it, and that he'd miss me and that he thought about not going because of me.

"That would be crazy, though," I said.

And he said, "I've been crazy before."

* * *

The week went by fast. George and I spent each night together, and each day he had a lot of errands to do and loose ends to tie up. One afternoon we were downtown and I wanted to get to the credit union before it closed to deposit my paycheck and he had to go buy a new pair of sunglasses, and we decided we'd meet back at his house in twenty minutes, but when I got there he hadn't gotten back yet. I waited around by the porch, because neither Marco or Anita were home and the door was locked. I waited and waited, and I started to wonder what was taking him so long.

Then it started raining. I didn't have my umbrella with me and there was barely any overhang on the porch, so it rained on me and I was getting cold. And then I started getting really mad at having to wait there. I thought that the least George could do was hurry up a little, because how long did it take to buy a pair of sunglasses anyway? I even imagined him running into a friend and going off to have a beer. It seemed like I was waiting so long that he was never going to show up, and then finally I saw him coming, jogging up the street with his hands in his pockets, and by the time he got to the door and was getting out his keys I was so mad I didn't even want to go inside anymore.

And he goes, "Hey, I--"

"What took you so long?"

"Yeah, the store--"

I didn't even wait for him to finish. "Because I've been standing here for like half an hour." I wasn't yelling, but my voice came out louder than usual, and he looked at me totally shocked, because he'd never even seen me mad before.

"You just let me stand out here in the rain, I've just been standing here all this time--" And even as I was saying it I knew how ridiculous it sounded, but all of a sudden I was so furious I couldn't even help it. I just said, "Where were you? Where were you?"

He goes, "Talia... Talia, let's go inside." He unlocked the door and we stood there in the living room dripping. I was still fuming, and he made me take my coat off and go sit on his bed while he got a towel for me to dry my hair. He sat down next to me, and he said he was sorry, that there was this huge long line at the store and an issue with the cash register, and he was sorry it took so long. But I knew it was so ridiculous that I didn't even care anymore, and I just felt like crying, or biting through something with all my might, and then I did start crying. George looked helpless, like he didn't know what to do with me, and I got angry at myself for being ridiculous. My nose was running and I was wiping at it and he was nice enough to go get me a tissue, and for a minute that made me cry even harder.

Then we sat there a long time without saying anything, and finally he leaned toward me and kissed me on the shoulder and I wasn't mad anymore, just hollowed out and really sad and I didn't want him to leave. Then I leaned toward him and let myself tip over, and he wrapped his arms around me, and we just stayed like that.

Finally, he said, "Please don't hate me for going."

I said, "I won't."

"Even if I deserve it."

"Okay."

* * *

A couple of nights later it wasn't raining and we drove out to the boatyard to sleep by the water. I brought a copy of J.D. Salinger's *Nine Stories* that I found at a used bookstore and we took turns reading aloud from it with a flashlight. I'd read it before, but I planned to give it to George to take with him. While he was reading the one about the soldier and the little girl I hugged him from behind and started listening more to his voice than the story.

His voice was like a warm blanket, and when I thought how I wouldn't be hearing it for so long my heart sliced in two. I kissed the back of his neck and I kissed him between the shoulder blades, and pretty soon he put down the book and switched off the flashlight and turned to face me. When we kissed he felt the tears on my cheeks, and he rubbed them with his thumb and he said, "Hey... Hey..."

And then we were kissing furiously, desperate, and I pulled him on top of me and we made the truck rock like a boat, and the night was like a hand, with us in its wide, dark palm.

* * *

In the morning I woke up before the sun rose. The sky was streaked with pink and the mist lying over the water was all pink too. George was still sleeping. I took the *Nine Stories* book and a pen and walked down the pier and sat on the end, and I drew a picture of a sailboat on one of the blank pages and on the sail I drew one of those hearts with an arrow through it.

In a little while George came down looking for me. He was sleepy-eyed and his hair was sticking up and he had one of the blankets wrapped around his shoulders, and he said, "There you are." He sat down and wrapped the blanket around both of us. He said, "I was afraid you'd disappeared."

13

The last night was at my place. In the morning he had to leave early, six o'clock, because he had to pick up Marco to go with him to the airport in Seattle.

I stood at the door with him, me in my pajamas and him with his backpack, and he put his arms around me and he whispered my name.

I said, "Come back soon."

And he said, "I will," even though we both knew it wouldn't be soon.

And we said I love you and we kissed and it was like stepping on glass. Then he went out the door and it closed behind him and I wanted to run after him, but I didn't.

I went back in my room and sat on my bed for an hour, crying. Finally, I got up and took a shower and got dressed and tried to eat a bowl of granola, because in not that long I had class. I didn't know how I'd make it through a class right then, but if I skipped it I didn't know what else I'd do.

Renee came in the kitchen and noticed my red eyes. She sat next to me. "George?"

I nodded and she held my hand for a while. Then she looked at my granola and said, "Can I have some of that?"

"For sure."

I blew my nose in the bathroom and when I came back she'd helped herself to a bowl. She lifted it up like she wanted to clink it to mine, and we did, and we said, "Cheers," at the same time.

I got through the day. After class I went to the library to read but I just kept reading the same line over and over and finally I gave up. I walked around campus and after a while I saw Calvin in the college activities building and he asked me what I was doing. I said, "Wandering aimlessly," which was what he usually said when I bumped into him outside of work. We hung out in some arm chairs by a window and when I didn't say much he gave me a little punch on the arm. I said, "Don't mind me."

But he said, "Sister, I've been there."

* * *

That night when I went into my room to get ready for bed the lamp on my night table was on, and underneath it I found a stack of five black and white photographs. Me and George. In one of the photos George was laughing, and in another he was kissing my cheek. I knew Renee had left them there and I thought, *What a nice thing to do.*

I tiptoed over to her room, and saw the light under the door so I knew she was still awake. I knocked and she said, "Come in," and I told her thank you, and she smiled and said, "You're welcome."

I sat on the foot of her bed and she looked at me over the top of her reading glasses. "You'll get used to it, you know. George being away."

I didn't know if I would or not, but I figured she would know better than me. I nodded. "For sure."

"Four months isn't a long time, in the scheme of things."

"You're right."

"And it will be really fun when he comes back."

"It will."

Then she goes, "And keep your pants up."

"What?"

"Don't let your butt hang out."

I burst out laughing. "What are you talking about?"

She started laughing too. "Just don't let it hang out."

I grabbed the extra pillow on her bed and threw it at her. "I thought you said *I* was the weird one."

She was laughing into the pillow now. "You are. You totally are."

A few days later it was my birthday. I was nineteen. George had left me a present that he wouldn't let me open until the day and when I woke up in the morning that was the first thing I did. It was a small brown box tied with a white string and inside there was a square of cotton and under that a sky-blue stone carved in the shape of a heart. It was polished smooth and had tiny white and green spots that made it look like the ocean. I kept it under my pillow, and a couple of times I fell asleep holding it.

I missed George with a physical ache. I kept his copy of *One Flew Over the Cuckoo's Nest* under my pillow along with the heart stone, because when I'd finished it and told him how much I liked it he'd said I should keep it, and he wrote on the first page, *For Talia, Love George*. I still wore the cord with his sailing knots in it, and every time I thought about him I gave it a tug.

* * *

George had given me an address in Mexico where he'd be able to get mail, and I wrote him letters with envelopes decorated in collage and paint. He wrote back, letters full of lurid details about the jungle landscape and brilliant seascape, the other crew members and passengers and their intrigues, huge insects and spiny fish and fruit that looked like rolled up armadillos. I loved the way he described things and I wrote to him that I thought his favorite authors must have rubbed off on him and that he should write a book about his adventures down there. When he wrote back he said maybe he'd write a book, but it would just be for me.

Twice, George called and we were able to talk on the phone. The calls were brief and full of static. Whatever conditions there were between us, and the thousands of miles of wires, they didn't work super well, and his voice sounded distant. But it was still him, it was still George, and then I knew he was still out there. He was real.

At the end of the first call I said, "I love you."

And he said, "Say it again. I just want to hear you keep saying it."

And at the end of the second call, when he said he loved me, I said, "Say it again, say it again."

In his letters, George said that he wished I was there with him and sometimes I wished I was too, but after a while, as much as I missed him, I was glad I was where I was, there at school. Though at night I had the most doubts, because that was when I missed him the most. I lay in bed in the dark, aching for his arms around me and his voice in my ear, and the old agony stole back in, and then there was no remedy but to imagine he was there and do it for myself, and sometimes I even put that in my letters.

* * *

One night I dreamed I was in a place with water all around. The water was warm and I was swimming through it, a tadpole sprouting legs, with the flat tail of an eel going back and forth, and when I broke the surface into the air the light shattered like glass. George was there, in a boat with a plywood camper shell, and he was sailing away and as he was about to go over the horizon, he said, "Don't forget me!"

He got further away and further away, and it hurt all over again, but I knew I couldn't go with him, I had to stay, my place and his place weren't the same.

I woke up saying, "I won't forget you." I said it to the empty air. I was there alone, but it was okay, because even though it was a sad dream, I was okay being just me. I was there and George was far away, and I could live with it. I fell asleep again wondering why George told me not to forget him. I thought he would know that I never would.

PART THREE

14

It was the middle of May and warm breezes were blowing. I passed by the athletic fields to the building with the mailboxes and there was a letter from George, and I was so happy I hugged it to my chest and opened it right away. But as I read it, standing there next to the silver grid of mailboxes with the little door of mine still hanging open, my mood started to change.

George wrote that one of the crew had gotten a wrist injury, and because of that his trip was getting extended a few more months, that he'd have more responsibility and that would be good for his future. He said it was a hard decision, a killer decision, and that he wouldn't have any qualms about it except for me, and that he wouldn't ever want to hurt me. He wrote, *I hope you'll wait for me, but I don't think it would be fair for me to expect you to.*

I closed my mailbox and went outside to sit on the steps. I read the letter over again. George was extending his trip for a few months, I grasped that slowly, but what did that even mean? Instead of coming back in the summer it would be sometime next fall? I didn't understand why he would do this. He said it was good for his future but I'd thought he missed me. If he could so easily decide to stay away for so long, did he really miss me? I felt like a big hand was crushing me down into the cement stairs.

And what did he mean by not expecting me to wait? Later on, when I had the chance I showed the letter to Renee. Renee said he meant exactly what he was saying, that he didn't expect me to wait, if I decided to see other people, and this really shook me up inside.

That night lying in bed I reread George's letter one more time. I started thinking that if he was extending his trip now, maybe he'd keep on extending it. I was pretty familiar with broken promises. Plans changed all the time when I was a kid, all the times we moved, all the people I never saw again. Just because you loved someone didn't mean you got to keep them.

I started thinking that maybe *he* was the one having doubts about us. Maybe *he* wanted to see other people, that maybe there was a woman on the boat. With my hands shaking I got out my notebook and I wrote a letter back saying that I didn't want to see anyone else, but that if he had changed his mind about us he should tell me right away. I even skipped class the next day so I could go to the post office and mail it as soon as possible.

* * *

I had no way of calling him and the mail was so slow and as the weeks passed by and there was no letter back from him, no call, without even meaning to I started to become convinced that he had changed his mind. That he didn't love me. A voice in my mind told me that his absence was proof of it, and the more I thought about it the more I was poisoned by the idea. A cold curtain of dread lowered down around me and I felt sick.

It was much worse than when he left. For days I had bees everywhere, in my stomach, in my head, shooting out my ears and tangling up in my hair. Half the time I walked around forgetting where I was going and what I was doing, and the other half I spent messing up at work and doing poorly with assignments. Plus, I was fighting with myself. I was supposed to be independent, I wasn't supposed to let a guy be my reason for being happy or not, but I was a mess. I was being weak.

Then one night when I let a pot of broccoli burn on the stove, Renee cornered me in my room. I was sitting on the floor, reading, and she braced her elbows on the doorframe.

"What the fuck is wrong with you?"

"What?" I'd been absorbed in my book for the moment, but now my stomach twisted.

"You heard me."

I stared at her feet. "Nothing." I couldn't tell her about my weakness, I was too ashamed of it.

"No, it's not nothing. You've been, like, furtive and sneaky, and way too quiet."

A sickly cord of heat shot up from my gut to my ears, and right then I had this weird flash of memory, of me and my mom fighting when I was little. I was trying to keep her out of my bedroom and screaming because I couldn't stand it anymore. But I also couldn't stand being alone in my room, and the two opposites were ripping me apart.

Renee was standing there, glaring.

I said, "I really don't want to talk right now."

She stared at me for a second more, then she walked away.

* * *

I thought I would hear back from George in at least two weeks. I thought maybe he'd write and things would be clearer and go back to the way they were before, but two weeks went by, then three, and then four, and nothing. And when I still didn't hear from George I started to get angry. Every time I checked the mailbox and there was nothing and every time the phone rang and it wasn't him that voice rose up in my mind saying, *You lied*. And something in my heart started to close down.

Inside I was raw, but outside my shell was hardening and this helped steady me, and I thought that anything was better than the confusion. I was coming out of a fog and now the light was brighter and harsher. Tables and chairs and windows had sharper angles and the hands of clocks stabbed at their own faces. After making a habit of holing up in my room I started going out again, a lot, and one Friday at work Calvin said he and his roommates were having a party that night and that I should come.

He said, "We gotta get you out of your funk."

That cracked my shell. He was so nice I wanted to hug him, because even while I was being so weird and messed up he still wanted to be my friend. And even though I didn't really want to go to the party I said I would.

* * *

I walked over around nine. I would have asked Renee if she wanted to go with me but she was hanging out with the soccer crowd so I went by myself. The door to Calvin's place was open and there were already quite a few people there—a handful from Media Loan, others from Calvin's film class, random friends and roommates, and on the stereo Aretha Franklin was playing, which always made me feel better, especially since I felt like my own chain of fools.

Calvin was in the kitchen serving up red wine with chunks of fruit in it, and he goes, "Hey party girl." He handed me a glass, smiling. "Sangria. You might not believe it, but this is my grandma's recipe."

I said, "Thanks Grandma." I didn't know if I wanted to drink it, but I carried it around with me and got into a couple of conversations, hoping maybe people would start dancing. That would have cheered me up, but no one was making a move in that direction and I didn't feel up to being the instigator, even if I was beginning to feel insanely restless.

I thought I'd see what kind of music they had lying around the stereo and I saw Calvin's roommate Toby sitting on one of the couches. He was holding a beer in his lap and had one foot up on the coffee table and he wasn't talking to anyone, so I decided to go say hi. We'd been pretty friendly ever since Halloween.

I sat down on the floor and put my drink on the coffee table. "Hey."

He goes, "Oh. Talia. Hi."

I said, "How's it going?"

He shrugged his shoulders. "Not too bad. How about you?"

I shrugged my shoulders too, that about summed it up.

He said, "I'm not in much of a party mood, actually." He put his beer down next to my drink and got up. "I think I might just take a walk."

That sounded nice. I was twitchy all over, and even though I figured he'd probably want to be alone, I said, "Do you mind company?"

And he said, "No, I wouldn't mind at all."

He said he wanted to get his coat and while he went in his room I leaned on the wall by the front door. I could see a bit into his room from there and I caught sight of a wooden box with strings on it, on his night table, and when he came out I said, "What's that box?"

He goes, "Oh that? I'll show you." He picked it up and put it in my hands. It was an instrument, the wood shiny and polished and with guitar strings stretched over an S-shaped hole. He said, "I made it last fall but I haven't figured out how to play it yet."

I plucked a few of the strings and gave it back to him. "It's nice."

"Thanks."

Toby put his coat on and we stepped outside. It was drizzling, but not too cold, and after we walked for a while I said, "So why aren't you in a party mood?" He didn't answer right away. "I mean, don't say, if it's too personal."

But he said, "No, it's okay. It's just…" He took off his baseball cap, which was backwards as usual, kind of rubbed his hair and put it back on. "Amanda and I broke up a couple days ago. So." He shrugged again.

I looked at the wet pavement passing under our feet. Maybe I sort of knew how he felt. I said, "I'm sorry."

He blew out some air. "Yeah. I guess it's for the best though."

"Really?"

He half-laughed. "That's what she says."

I didn't know Amanda, but I wondered why she would think that, especially about someone as cool as Toby, but people did change their minds, and that thought twisted a little dagger in my heart.

We were passing by the back of the rec center where there were a bunch of stairs and I was still feeling extremely restless so I started running up and down them.

Toby goes, "You look like you've had too much coffee."

I said, "I just need to get some energy out." I was already breathing harder.

And he said, "If you want to run up stairs we should go over to the clock tower."

I said, "Clock tower, yes!" Toby laughed. I laughed too. Moving around was lifting my mood.

He said, "Race ya!" and left me in the dust. I wasn't that fast of a runner, but I got there eventually and we both ran up the six flights of the clock tower, up to the locked door where the enclosed part of the staircase began. I'd been all the way to the top once before, on a tour my very first week at college—you could see for hundreds of miles—but you had to have a key.

We stood there panting, our breath making big clouds of steam, and I slapped my hands on the door. The metal was painted a sickly brownish green and I said, "I hate this color."

Toby laughed again. "How is that pertinent?"

I laughed too, but then all of a sudden I was genuinely angry. I said, "Because this door is locked and I want to go all the way up and this awful color is here in my face, mocking me."

I knew I wasn't making any sense, but Toby surprised me by saying, "Actually, I think I know what you mean." Then he said, "Let's find better stairs."

We ran up the stairs by the bus roundabout, down the ones by the communications building, and kept walking wherever, and finally went back to our area of the dorms. The party at Toby and Calvin's had died down and I said, "Looks like it's safe to go in."

"Yeah," Toby yawned. "What are you going to do?"

I yawned too. "I'm going to bed."

He said, "Sleep good."

"You too."

15

The next couple weeks I saw Toby several times at Media Loan. He was working on a composition and kept checking out four-track tape recorders and different kinds of microphones and keys for the editing suites. If it wasn't too busy we'd talk about what he was working on, or the ethnography project I was doing with a couple classmates, or any good stairs we had been on lately. He said he liked the stairwell in the communications building because it had a really good echo. Once I asked him if he'd figured out how to play his homemade instrument.

He said, "Not yet."

I said, "Maybe you can work it into a composition."

And he said, "That's not a bad idea."

* * *

Things were getting more complicated for Renee. She'd forgiven me for "going underground," as she called it, and we'd resumed our usual talks. Dylan, the assistant soccer coach, was figuring in as a more prominent subject, because their relationship had gotten more than social. These days he stayed over with Renee pretty frequently, and one Sunday afternoon when Renee and I had been reading on the couches for hours, she put down her book and said, "Do you want to help me reorganize my closet?"

My eyes were about to fall out from reading so much and my brain was so stuffed with words I thought there was no more room left, so I put down my book too and said yes.

Once we were in Renee's room we started moving the boxes from the bottom of her closet out to the middle of the floor. Alec's photo watched us from the wall and I said, "You're spending a lot of time with Dylan now."

She said, "Hella lot of time."

I looked at Alec's photo and she guessed what I was wondering. She said, "It's inevitable. I mean, you think Alec's not meeting any girls down at Reed?" She rolled her eyes. "You can't marry your high school boyfriend." Then she turned around and started throwing things out of her closet and onto her bed. I watched the pile growing, feeling uneasy. I could tell she was upset and I wished I had something helpful to say, but I was way out of my depth.

I started to ask her if she wanted me to fold clothes or anything, but she was too busy ripping things off hangers and grabbing stuff from the top shelf. Finally, when the closet was completely excavated and the bed was heaped up like an avalanche, she flopped down right on top of the pile and rubbed her eyes. She said, "I still love Alec, though. I don't think that's going to change."

* * *

Calvin kind of pulled me aside one Friday during our shift. He goes, "Toby was asking about you."

130 EIGHTEEN

"What do you mean?"

"He asked me what the deal was with your boyfriend."

"George?"

He waited.

I said, "What did you say?"

Calvin said, "I said he should ask you."

I said, "I'm not sure myself, to tell the truth."

Then Calvin said, "Toby's a really good friend."

I didn't know what Calvin meant by saying that, but I said, "He seems like it."

* * *

The next time Toby came into Media Loan he told me he had an idea he wanted to try, a recording he wanted to make in the communications building stairwell, but he needed another person to help.

He said, "Do you think you might be up for it? It wouldn't take that long, maybe twenty minutes."

"For sure."

"Tonight okay? I want to go when it's empty."

"Sure." We both smiled.

* * *

At about eight o'clock Toby came by my place and we headed over to the stairwell. It was still light out but the clumps of forest by the walking path were dark with shadows and birds were calling in the branches. There was this one kind of call you often heard in the evenings, a sing-song sound that lasted forever and trailed off in an echoey kind of trill, and I said, "I've always wondered what bird that is."

"Swainson's thrush," Toby said.

"How do you know that?" I was pretty surprised, but he said he had a couple of ornithology friends. He said the Swainson's thrush always gave him chills and that he'd tried to record it before but it never came out right.

* * *

Once we got inside the stairwell all the natural light was shut out. It was lit enough to see but pretty dark in the corners, and the concrete walls rose so high you almost couldn't see the ceiling. Besides the four-track, a mic and an extremely long cable, Toby had the box instrument he made which he set down on the very bottom floor. He asked me to go up a few flights with the equipment and slowly lower the mic down on the cable toward him while he played it.

When I was up high enough, Toby started picking out a little melody on the strings and I started lowering the mic. The wood of the instrument made the notes resonate and the echo in the stairwell expanded the sound. I watched, leaning over the railing, trying to let the mic down smoothly so it didn't swing too much. We ended up staying in there for hours because he wanted to try it different ways and we both kept having ideas.

Finally, we finished up and walked back to the dorms. We stopped outside my building.

Toby said, "Thanks a lot for helping me."

"It was really fun."

Then he held his arms out. "Group hug?" I laughed and we hugged. It was brief, but I hadn't really hugged anyone since George had left and I felt a rush, like my body suddenly jumped back into living. Toby's arms were warm and solid and I felt his breath on my neck for a second, and then his eyes and his heavy brows were up close and my face flushed.

I said, "G'night."

"Night."

I went inside and got to bed with my body buzzing and my mind not knowing which way was up. I could still hear the melody Toby had been playing and that night it was sort of my lullaby.

16

By the last week of classes the days were amazingly long. It was still twilight by ten o'clock, and one night when I was in my room Toby tapped at the window. It was partially open but I slid it open the rest of the way.

He said, "Stairs?"

That had become our code word for taking walks. I guess we'd been taking a lot of walks.

And then it was evaluation week, and I was finishing all my projects and papers, and Renee was spending whole nights in the computer lab writing, and Tuesday night, after I'd gotten home from my dance exam, Toby came by with a cassette tape in his hand.

He said, "I finished it." He looked pretty excited.

"Can I hear it?"

"Have time right now?"

We sat on the floor in my room next to my boom box and he put in the tape. He said, "It's about twelve minutes."

I hugged my knees, leaned my forehead on them and closed my eyes. The piece started with a fluttering kind of beat and then ambient sounds layered in, then the melody, and it built up and then shifted, evolving slowly so that new elements came in, voices and footsteps, even a snippet of me laughing. New sounds came up and old ones faded out without you really realizing, but it was like a journey, a river of sound with a central heartbeat and an overarching song.

When it finished I said, "I love it."

His face kind of lit up. "Do you?"

"I totally do. Can you play it again?"

He rewound the tape and pressed play. Then he held out his hand, like he was going to shake my hand as thanks for my congratulations. And we shook hands, but then he didn't let go, and then I didn't let go, and the music took over the room.

I was sick of feeling unwanted. All those days of not knowing if I'd get a letter or a call from George, not knowing if he'd ever come back, all those nights alone with the bed feeling like the dark side of the moon. And there Toby was, being a good friend, holding my hand in his warm hand, his auburn eyes looking deeper, seeing something in my heart that maybe I saw in his too. And if there was anything still keeping me away, still keeping the door propped open for George, the music broke it, and I let my face turn toward Toby's, and for better or worse I crossed the line.

* * *

Toby stayed that night and every night for the rest of evaluation week. Then he went home to Spokane and Renee drove back to Berkeley and Calvin left to spend the summer in Seattle, and I moved into a dilapidated student house on the East Side where one of Renee's boomerang friends lived, and the school year turned into summer.

I stayed working at Media Loan but once again everything else was different: the house, people I didn't know, no classes, the weather had changed, and a lot of the time I felt like a stranger in my own life. Renee had Berkeley to go back to and Toby was happy to visit Spokane, and George was still in Mexico pursuing his dream which now had nothing to do with me, and it seemed like it was my lot to always be a stranger.

And the truth was I still missed George. I tried so hard not to, and I'd even succeeded for long stretches, especially when I was with Toby, and I told myself I was an idiot for missing someone who didn't miss me, that that was the most idiotic kind of person in the world.

Even so, things slowly got better. I started getting to know my new housemates and I liked them, especially Hafsa, who was a few years older and had just graduated and played the accordion and was working downtown at a hot tub place while she figured out what to do next. Amy had sent me another book she said I couldn't live without, *Catch-22*, and I stayed up late every night reading it. The night I read that Milo Minderbinder sold chocolate-covered cotton to his own squadron I laughed out loud, and my housemate, Tom, called out, "What's so funny?" through the wall. I even got some hours doing yard work for extra money and I thought maybe I'd get over everything and feel like a version of myself again.

At the end of July, Toby came back and stayed for a week, and even if things weren't so intense like they'd been with George, being with him was a long thirsty drink of water, and it kept my mind out of its dark alleys. Beefy, red-haired Tom spent his free time rock climbing and did pull-ups on the doorframe with his fingertips. He was from Spokane, like Toby, and they discovered they knew several people in common.

In the middle of that week, late one afternoon when Hafsa was on the porch practicing accordion and Toby and I were lying in the hammock in the grown-over front yard, Tom came home and sat in the grass and started taking off his boots. He'd been working construction all summer and he goes, "Man. My socks have been getting so dirty I just want to throw them away."

And I don't know why, but that struck me as so funny and I laughed so hard that Hafsa stopped playing, and Toby started laughing because I was laughing and he goes, "You're going to make us fall out," and I just hugged him around the waist and kept laughing.

Hafsa tended to say things in a very deadpan manner and I heard her say, "Talia thought that was very funny." And Toby hugged me back and I pressed my face into his chest and I just thought, *I'm going to live. I'm going to live.*

Then the week was over and Toby left for New York to do an internship at some studio for a month, and I was by myself again. I made tapes for Amy with Media Loan equipment, I made a little video of Hafsa playing her accordion while Tom did these very funny clumsy handstands in the yard, and I still kept thinking, *I'm going to live.*

* * *

But while Toby was in New York I got two letters from George. They were dated a month apart but arrived on the same day, and I sat with them on my bed a long time without opening them. Finally, I tore the envelopes and unfolded the pages and read them, the whole time saying to myself that I wasn't George's anymore and he wasn't mine, and I didn't know what to feel. He said he would most likely be back in October, and one second I was angry that he couldn't even tell me that for sure, and the next second I was hit by this vicious wave of shame, because I'd told him I didn't want to see anyone else and gone and done the opposite, and he didn't even know it yet.

I lay on my bed and curled up. The sun was low in the sky and I could hear kids playing in the park across the street, a dog barking, and my housemates downstairs talking in the kitchen. I closed my eyes and put my hands on my stomach. The bees were going in there and I was sure they were trying to kill me.

* * *

Much later I sat on the porch with a box of cornflakes, because I knew I had to eat something for dinner and that was the best I could do. I had shorts on and I started looking at the two little scars on my kneecaps, one from falling off a bike when I was a kid, and one from falling on an escalator, and that made me start thinking about the scar on George's back.

A few times, back in the early part of the spring, George was sore from work because he'd been on a job with a lot of extra lifting, and when I told him I had a knack for giving massages he said he'd pay me money, and I'd said, "Please shut up about that." And he'd lie on the bed with his shirt off and I'd dig my hands into his back muscles and he'd groan and say, "So good..." And I'd laugh.

The first time I gave him a massage like that I noticed this scar on his back I hadn't seen before, a jagged white line next to the middle of his spine about two inches long. When I asked about it he said it was from an accident he'd had swimming the summer he was twelve. He said it was right before his dad left, and they'd all gone up to a lake for a few days, but his parents weren't getting along. He tried to swim under this floating dock on the lake and scraped against a piece of metal that was sticking out and came out of the water gushing blood.

When he got back to the shore Paulo spotted him and started screaming and then his mom came running and they eventually got him to an emergency room in a nearby town where a couple of nurses stitched him up. And it wouldn't have been too bad, but his parents got into a terrific fight afterward and his dad left to go back to Bellingham and soon after that left for good.

George said he never got the whole story on why his dad left but he had the impression that his dad had started seeing another woman. After the divorce his mom was pretty careful not to talk badly about him to George and Paulo because she didn't want to damage their relationship with him. George said she would probably tell him now what happened if he wanted to know, but he didn't actually really want to know.

After George told me that story I looked at the scar again and of course I started kissing it. I could just see him as a kid, lying in bed all bandaged up, listening to his parents fight downstairs, and I just kept kissing him there.

George said, "I'm getting pretty jealous of that spot."

I laughed and said I'd fix that.

* * *

My confusion was coming back, and like the black widows in the woodpile, evil little surprises occasionally popped up and stung me. Like the day I was at work and Millie put on a Zombies album. One of the nights just before George left for Mexico, we were at his house in the kitchen washing dishes, listening to a mix tape of sixties bands like the Animals and the Doors, and "Time of the Season" came on with that instrumental line *do-do-do-Ch-K-Ah! do-do-do-Ch-K-Ah!* George quit what he was doing and wrapped an arm around my waist and we started dancing to the song. He pulled me so close and I put my forehead into the crook of his shoulder and my hand on his neck and he led the dance with his hips, and I just didn't want it to end. And then when I suddenly heard that song in the middle of my workday, right when I was hefting a monitor up onto a shelf, I got this terrible squeezing in my throat and I walked straight out the door and to the bathroom down the hall, and I stood in a stall trying to pull myself together.

When I came back, my boss, Millie, said,

"Everything okay?" And I said yes. But I wasn't really. Not for the whole rest of the day.

17

The night Toby came back from New York we went to bed almost right away. I was so glad he was back, but something was off. He kissed me in an impatient way and his smile wasn't as warm as usual, and afterward when we were lying there I asked him if anything was wrong.

He said, "No, nothing's wrong."

I said, "You're acting different."

He was quiet a long time, and I said, "Toby..."

And he took a big breath and said, "I sort of hooked up with someone. A girl in New York."

I choked for a second. "What do you mean, hooked up?"

When he didn't answer, I said, "You slept with her?" And when he didn't answer that, I said, "Okay." I was dizzy. I didn't want to be naked anymore and I got up and started putting my pajamas on, but I was having a hard time breathing.

Toby said, "Talia, it didn't mean anything. It was one time, it was just a fling." I knew from his voice he was worried and when I sat back down on the bed he kind of hugged my arm and said, "I'm scrry. I messed up. I'm sorry."

I wasn't putting my thoughts together very well, but I couldn't say he'd done anything wrong exactly. Technically we'd only been together for two weeks, if you added it up, and we hadn't made any promises.

I said, "Where does this leave us?"

He said, "I still want to see you. It was just a fling, I'm serious."

I lay down and closed my eyes. I didn't fault him because hadn't I done worse myself? I thought, *I deserve this.*

Toby put his head by my shoulder and curled up around me. "I still want to be with you." And a minute later, "It won't happen again."

I believed him. Or at least I believed he meant it when he said it, just like I'd believed everything George had said, and everything I'd said. But people did change their minds, it happened all the time, and there was no way to know anything for sure.

Toby was no worse than me, in fact he was better, because I hadn't even told George about him. I hadn't written back yet, I was too scared. Not that I hadn't tried. I'd sat down several times with a pen and paper, but either I wrote nothing or I wrote something that sounded too horrible and threw it away.

* * *

And then it was September. Renee's boomerang friend moved out of our house and Renee took over his room and I was pretty thrilled we were living together again. Toby had moved into a house not far away with Calvin and a couple of their friends and despite the New York fling I knew he cared about us because he wanted to hang out a lot and was a big cuddler.

And he was *there*. I could see him and feel him and smell him and touch him and he wasn't going away, and that was a lot more than I could say for George. And then classes started up and the mornings turned cold and finally I did write the letter.

I wrote that I hoped things were going well for him in Mexico, and I said I'd been hanging out a lot with Calvin's roommate, Toby. It was a bullshit letter but I couldn't do any better. I was terrified George would be hurt and I was also terrified he wouldn't care, and once again a pair of opposites was tearing me apart. When I finished I could barely seal the envelope, I was shaking so badly, and I ran almost the whole way to the post office before I changed my mind. My throat was raw when I got there, and I had a horrible side ache, and after the letter left my hands I twisted my ankle on the curb and honestly, at that moment, if a bus had run me over I wouldn't have cared.

So, the letter went out, addressed to George in Mexico, and I never heard anything back. Nothing at all.

* * *

I had this memory from when I was a kid, the summer I stayed in Berkeley with my dad after my mom and I had moved up to Ukiah. My dad lived in a collective house and this one guy, Steve, was together with this woman Judy who lived there too. Steve had gone to Alaska to work on a fishing boat and while he was away Judy got together with another housemate, Phil. Then Steve was coming back and we all drove to the airport together to pick him up.

I was nine years old, just a kid, and I didn't know anything about anything, but I knew that Judy and Phil were nervous about telling Steve what was going on. I was walking along in the airport next to Judy in those giant bright corridors, and I said, "I don't envy your position, Judy."

She laughed. "God, Talia. You and your one-liners."

And then we were waiting and the plane arrived and Steve got out with his big backpack on and looking like a wild man, and everyone hugged. Then we got to the parking lot and climbed in the van, and the beans got spilled right away. Steve asked Phil how his summer was going and Phil goes, "Good, well, things are going good at work... and I got a new lover..." And then he looked at Judy and then Steve knew, and there was this silence, and then Steve started crying and no one said a word.

It wasn't that I imagined George reacting like that. I had no idea at all. I was nineteen now, but so often I still felt like a kid, like I didn't know anything about anything. All I knew was that September passed by and then it was October, and it got cold and the leaves fell and classes stacked up and papers were due, and I still didn't hear anything from George, and anytime I thought about him I just felt afraid.

* * *

Then a couple of weeks before Halloween I was at home in the kitchen and the phone rang, and when I answered I heard, "Hey, Talia, it's Anita."

I was so surprised, I hadn't even seen her since the spring, but then I thought she must be calling about George and I got this bolt of fear. She said he was back, and that he was staying with her and Marco for a couple of days to take care of a few things.

She said, "He told me you've been seeing someone else." And when I didn't say anything, she said, "Talia, he's pretty broken up about it."

I gripped the phone. Maybe I'd been wrong about him not caring. I must have been wrong.

Anita said, "He's going to be staying with his brother for a while. I don't think he's sticking around here."

I said, "Was he not planning to call me?"

"I don't think so. That's why I'm letting you know, in case you want to see him."

"I do," I said. "I do want to see him. Thanks for telling me."

She said, "Come tomorrow night, if you want. He'll be here."

"I will."

* * *

I went after I got off work. I took the bus from campus to the house and I was so scared to see him that the whole way over I thought I was going to jump out the window, and when I got there and knocked on the door, I was shaking.

Marco opened the door and said, "Hey, Talia, I'll tell George you're here." And I sat on the couch, not knowing what I'd say. Then I heard footsteps. George was coming down the hall and I almost didn't recognize him.

His hair was long and wild and his skin was dark from all that time in the sun and his beard was quite grown out, and he had this thick scarf around his neck that I'd never seen, but what shocked me most were his eyes. His eyes looked cold and far away, and I felt like I was looking at a stranger.

He said, "Talia," and I got up and we hugged, but it was very awkward.

I said, "How are you? When did you get back?"

We talked a little and we sat on the couch but he hardly looked at me, and the longer I stayed the sadder I got, and the worse I felt that I'd betrayed him, and it seemed like whatever we'd had before was broken now, on a trash heap somewhere, and it didn't fit whatever shape I'd thought my heart had grown into.

He said he was moving to Bellingham, that because of Mexico he had the money and experience he needed to start a charter boat business with Paulo, just like they'd always wanted. He said, "It's kind of a dream come true." But he didn't sound happy at all.

Everything was wrong. I couldn't say any of the things that I should have, the things that were real. All those things about me, about Toby, about George, it was a log jam, a tangle of branches like I used to see in Ukiah when the creek dried up in the summer. Storms had washed it all down and lodged it in the places where big rocks were close together, and there was no way in, no way to move it.

I said the worst thing then. I said, "I missed you." It was true, but it was wrong to say it.

George half-laughed. "Well, you didn't waste any time getting a replacement."

His words cut through me like a cold knife and I deserved it all.

And then there was nothing to do but go. I knew he didn't want me to stay.

I said good-bye to Marco and Anita and I asked George if we could stay in touch, and I don't know if he meant it, but he said, "Of course."

I said, "Bye, George." I knew he wouldn't hug me again.

"See ya."

And I left. I ran to the bus stop and when the bus came I went all the way in the back and put up my hood and cried my fucking eyes out.

* * *

I found Toby working in the communications building the next day. He started to give me hug but noticed my expression and asked me what was wrong.

"I saw George yesterday." And I told him I was feeling pretty confused.

He took my hand and led me to a private corner. "Hold on, what are you saying?"

"Nothing, I just talked to him for maybe half an hour. He's moving to Bellingham."

Toby leaned against the wall. "What are you confused about?"

I shook my head. I couldn't say, I didn't know. It was too many things at once.

"You're not over him, are you?"

"Please don't be mad." I didn't think I could handle two people hating my guts at the same time.

"But are you planning to see him or anything?"

"No. I'd be pretty surprised if we ever speak again."

And then, I didn't know why, but I asked him if he was still in touch with the girl from New York, even though I already thought that was over.

But he said, "Now and then."

That surprised me. "How often is that?"

He said he didn't know, but I pressed him, and he said once or twice a week, and that sounded like a lot to me.

I said, "Toby, what are we doing?"

"I thought we were dating. What do you think we're doing?"

"I'm not sure anymore."

18

I thought a lot about Toby and a lot about George, and I tried to pick apart what I was feeling. I remembered this day from the previous spring when George and I were walking out by the boat yard and we walked down on the pier and I told him about going to the marina in Berkeley with one of the old housemates and her dog, and George said, "How many communes did you live in, anyway?"

I thought about it a minute. "Seven or eight, depending on what you count as a commune."

"All in Berkeley and Ukiah?"

"Most of them."

"Was that kind of chaotic for you?"

I hadn't thought about that before, I hadn't known anything different. I said, "I guess I was used to it."

George took my hand. "Did your parents ever talk to you about it?"

"No." All of a sudden I was crying a little bit.

He said, "Why do I get the feeling no one talked to you about your life?"

I said, "They weren't like that."

"Your parents?"

"It wasn't their concern. My mom especially, she had her own concerns."

"Like what?"

"I don't know, she was busy."

"Where did that leave you, then?"

I couldn't answer. No one had ever asked me those kinds of things before and I didn't understand what George was seeing or how he even guessed about it. Then I suppose he sensed I was struggling because he said, "I don't mean to be hounding you or anything." He said, "I hate the thought of you being lonely."

I wiped my eyes with my wrist. "Weren't you ever lonely growing up?"

"I guess. But I always had Paulo, and our mom took good care of us. She really kept it together after my dad left."

I said, "Good thing."

George brought his forehead to mine, said, "It was," and kissed me on the lips.

Toby wasn't one for talking about things like that too much. Once he said, "I think you're a little obsessed with the past." We were walking to the college activities building to buy something to eat, and I asked him what he meant and he said never mind.

I said, "My past is part of me. Is there something wrong with that?" He socked me on the arm, all playful, and said to forget it, that it was just a throw-away comment, but I didn't really find it funny.

* * *

Then a few nights before Halloween I got this crazy idea to call Hari in Los Angeles. We'd never even spoken on the phone, though I had a number in my address book, and the last time we'd exchanged letters was after the New Year's card I sent him several months ago.

I went down to the kitchen where the phone was. Everyone was in their rooms and the lights were off and I dialed the number. The phone rang at the other end and he actually picked up and I heard his gentle voice. "Sat Nam, Hari here."

"Hey, Hari, it's Talia."

"Talia? Hey, wow, are you calling from Washington?"

"I am, yeah." I kind of cleared my throat. "I hope it's not weird for me to be calling out of the blue."

"No, no, it's great to hear your voice."

I said it was great to hear his voice too and I asked how he was doing and how school was going and everything and he asked the same, and then I got up my nerve and I said, "Hari, can I ask your advice on something?"

And he goes, "Sure you can."

"Because I think you're the one person I can ask about this." I thought I might start crying.

"You can ask me anything you want."

So, I told him about George and I told him about Toby and being confused. I said I had been thinking about the very first conversation we ever had, at the yoga workshop, about peace and how he'd said he felt connected to his creator and how that guided him in his choices. I said he was still the only person I'd ever heard talk about things like that, and that that was the kind of guide I needed myself.

Hari was quiet for a while, then he said, "Well, I can tell you what my yoga teacher told me a couple of years ago, when I was deciding where to go for college. It was the first big decision I'd ever made, and she knew I was agonizing over it."

"What did she say?"

"She said I should try not thinking about it for a few days, and if the question came up in my mind I should say to myself that I was turning the decision over to the creator, and that at the end of the few days I would just know."

"Did it work?"

"It really did. After two days it was like a little voice was going, '*UCLA...UCLA...*'"

I laughed. "Straight from the mouth of the creator."

Hari laughed too, but then he said, "But decisions aren't always that straightforward, you know? Your situation might be more complicated than that."

"Also, I'm not sure I have a relationship with the creator." I wasn't laughing now. I didn't feel like a person who had that special relationship, not like Hari.

He said, "You don't have to call it that though, you can call it intuition or the universe, or whatever. In any case, there's guidance that's available to us. I really believe that. And it knows more than we do."

I leaned back against the kitchen wall, I could hear water dripping into the sink. "That's what I need, exactly, because sometimes I feel like I don't know anything." I liked the word intuition. I'd had intuitions before, but they were so random. I didn't know you could look for them on purpose.

"For me, I've found it really helps to spend some time getting quiet," Hari said. "I do that in the morning with my practices and my prayers in the evening, but if I'm really struggling with something I make even more time for it."

"Okay." I was hopeful now.

He said, "This might not make sense, but it's like I close my eyes and follow a tunnel down into myself and I feel around for what's really true."

* * *

So, I spent some time getting quiet like Hari said. Sometimes I walked out to the school farm and around its perimeter where I knew I wouldn't run into anyone, except maybe the chickens. Instead of thinking about Toby or George or the things I had to do for school or at home, I tried to pay attention to the ground under my feet and my breathing. There weren't any instant revelations or anything, but after walking I noticed I felt more settled than I had at first, even sort of calm.

One day I was walking between the vegetable beds at the farm that had been tarped over for the winter with black plastic, and I got this tight, crowded feeling in my chest. I thought about Toby, how I'd just seen him that morning because we'd ridden the bus to school together, and how he squeezed my hand when we went our separate ways. I stared at the drops of water that were sprinkled all over the black plastic and I got this sinking feeling that I had to break up with him.

It was strange because I really cared about Toby, maybe I loved him, even if it was a different kind of love than what I'd had with George. He was sweet and fun to be with and I had no complaints even if he talked to the girl from New York a lot. But it was growing clear to me that staying with Toby would never feel right, like if I put my right foot in my left shoe, and just tried to keep walking.

* * *

We got together to talk one evening over at his house. We sat on his bed and I had a pounding ache in my chest. He was leaning up against the wall, waiting for me to say something and finally I said, "You've been great--"

And he goes, "Oh, fuck, Talia..." because he knew what I was going to say, because he wasn't stupid, he'd kind of seen it coming. He grabbed the back of his neck and moved his head around like it hurt.

"I'm sorry."

He said, "Does this have anything to do with Tamara?"

I said no. I said I had to sort myself out.

I wondered all over again what the hell I was doing and why. It didn't make any real sense, especially when it wasn't like George was waiting in the wings, it wasn't like I was choosing between them.

I said, "I do think you're great, I mean it. You are." My voice was shaking, because I did mean it, and I thought, *Who am I to hurt people?* Two people. I was sick to my stomach.

And then Toby said he wanted me to go, and I left.

* * *

The weeks ticked by and I kept walking around the farm, or I went on bike rides on the quiet roads around the area, or down to the beach and walked along the rocky shore. Walking on the beach one day I remembered this time that George and I had gone. There was hardly any wind and the water was glassy and still.

We found a bunch of flat, round rocks that were good for skipping and we started throwing them in the water. I wasn't great at it, not like George was. His rocks skipped out so far that by the time they sunk you couldn't see them anymore. And I remembered how he touched my fingers and said I had pretty hands, and how he blew on them to get the sand off.

This time I was there alone. I looked around and found a flat, oval-shaped black stone that would have been perfect for skipping but I didn't try. I put it in my pocket and held it there with my hand, and I decided a second thing, which was to keep to myself for a while, as far as guys were concerned.

* * *

On Thanksgiving Day, Renee and Hafsa and Tom and I and a few friends made a big meal at our house, and we talked and laughed and hung out for hours telling funny stories and listening to music. Later, when it was dark, I took a walk by myself. I looked at my house from across the park, the living room windows lit up cozy and yellow. I thought about George up in Bellingham with

Paulo and their mom probably, and whoever else he might be celebrating with, and when I took a deep breath the sharp air stung my throat. I went around the block one more time, and when I got back to my front porch I decided I needed to write to him.

I wrote a short letter. I said I hoped he was doing well and that things were going good in his business with Paulo and I asked him to say hi to Paulo for me. I said a couple of things about school and I said that I wasn't seeing Toby anymore, for about a month now. I wanted to say I was sorry for what I did, but everything I tried still seemed wrong, so at the end of the letter I just wrote, "Miss you," and "Love, Talia."

But I never heard back from him.

19

Renee and I drove to California again for the winter break, but this time not with Alec. They'd gotten back together over the summer, but in the fall Renee had started seeing Dylan again. Things kept changing.

Ukiah wasn't so bad. My dad had been going through boxes of old papers he kept under his bed, and one evening he dragged something out saying, "Look what I found."

It was this big yellow kite with a cartoon face from *The Planet of the Apes* on it, that we used to take to parks around Berkeley to fly. I hadn't seen it in years.

I said, "Why don't we try it out?"

The next day we drove over and flew it on the football field of my old high school, and it was windy enough that it pulled way up, like a mile into the sky. The string was unrolled all the way and the kite was pulling for more. I was probably eight or nine the last time we'd flown it, and the last time I'd been on that field was two and a half years before at graduation, that surreal day where we all marched in to *Pomp and*

Circumstance and then sat roasting under the sun in our purple gowns during the speeches before going off to party after party.

My dad was looking up at the kite with his arms folded, probably calculating its exact height by considering the string as the hypotenuse of a giant right triangle. Now and then the kite flipped and turned in the wind and I would catch a glimpse of the ape face, far away. Right then I got the funny feeling that I was looking at my own face from a long, long distance, a tiny version of myself. A little ape fluttering high above the poplar trees waving at the edge of the field, high above the tar paper roofs of the houses beyond those, and I thought, *I do come from somewhere.*

* * *

I did the Christmas thing with my mom and Willow again too. One of Willow's daughters was up visiting with her two toddlers who ran around after the dogs, trying to grab their tails. They ate a lot of crackers and the dogs ran around after them eating the crumbs, and then they wanted me to read them all their storybooks. I sat on the couch with the little guys on either side of me and read the books over and over. Every time I finished one they'd throw another in my lap, and I laughed because they were so cute and so innocent. And my mom and I got along fine. She took a few pictures of me reading with the boys and she genuinely seemed glad I was there, and it made me think about how maybe things could get better with time.

Late in the afternoon I went walking on the dirt road that led from my mom's house to the gravel road that led into town. The sky was clear and the bare branches of the oaks spread out gray and brown with patches of pale green lichen. I thought about how George once told me what things were like with his dad after he left the family, when George was twelve years old.

We'd gone sailing on a warm day and were just drifting along and I asked him if he saw his dad very much after that, and he said not that much because he'd moved out of state. George said, "I was pretty mad at him for a long time."

He said the summer he was seventeen though, he and Paulo stayed with their dad for a month and they built a rowboat in the driveway. It was the first boat George ever worked on and he loved building it, so he owed that to his dad. He said, "It was the only thing the three of us could do without fighting."

I remembered the look on George's face when he'd said that, like he was still amazed.

It was starting to get dark out now, so I turned around and headed back to the house. Long before I got there I heard the dogs barking and the little boys yelling, they must have been out in the garden. I thought about how important things, things that might change your life, like rowboats, could be born out of difficulty, and I wondered if I'd ever talk to George again.

* * *

After Ukiah I spent several days in San Francisco with Amy. She hosted a New Year's party again and we made postcards, just like the year before, and I made a special one for Hari, thanking him for his advice and telling him how much it continued to help me. And even though George never wrote me back, I decided to make a card for him too, with a sailboat on it in a lot of reds and yellows and oranges, and I promised myself I wouldn't write again if he didn't answer this time. I wished him a happy 1991 and said a few other things and at the end I didn't write, "Miss you," but I did write, "Love, Talia."

A couple of weeks later when I was back at school I finally did hear from him.

He'd sent a postcard with lumberjacks on it, which was kind of funny, and said thanks for both my cards and that things were good and that he was seeing someone, a girl named Sherry, and at the end when he signed off he didn't say, "Love, George," he said, "Take care."

So, then I thought, *That's it. It's done.* He was moving on and I should too.

21

All January I kept up with my quiet times. Often when I walked I practiced my Orissi hand gestures. There were dozens we had to memorize, and it took practice to get them to flow from one to another. Dr. Sundara was teaching us a dance about Ganesh, the god with the elephant head, with gestures and movements that showed how he was the son of Shiva and Parvati and had a big belly and sat under an oak tree and was the best dancer. At the beginning, you came onto the stage holding flower petals in your hands as an offering, raining them down slowly to show reverence to Ganesh for removing the obstacles from your path. Then he was shown as a baby and a grown-up god, and how his mind had blossomed into enlightenment.

In dance class the music and the movement sucked me in, absorbing me into these other stories. It sort of put my own small story into a larger one, and even if there was pain, it came out in a beautiful way. And there was also so much power in it. Now that I was in the advanced level we got to use the ankle bells, strings of fifty brass bells on each ankle that were heavy and took getting used to. Striking the ground with the ball of your foot or the heel or a flat stamp made them crash and added percussion to the music. The arm movements flowed like water, but the footwork was quite forceful. I watched Dr. Sundara, how fierce and strong she was and how gracefully she moved, even when she wasn't dancing. I hoped that someday those qualities might grow in me.

And even though I was supposed to be moving on, even though he'd made things pretty clear, I was still thinking about George. When I took my walks and wasn't thinking about anything in particular, memories still surfaced, like those koi fish in ponds that rise up from the bottom and put their lips into the air. I remembered how George looked when he was sleeping, and dancing, and sailing, and laughing, and getting dressed, and eating and drinking a beer, and finally I stopped trying to make the memories go away.

* * *

One day around the first of February I took a walk to the farm between classes. There were patches of snow on the ground along the path and a few little puddles with ice over them and I kept stepping on the ice just to hear it crunch. And it was so quiet, except for the cracking ice and occasionally a cawing crow. There was one frozen puddle with a tree root going through the middle and I balanced one foot on the root for a second before bringing my heel down on the ice, and somewhere in between the balance and the crack I suddenly decided something else. I decided that I would go up to Bellingham and see George, if he'd see me, because I wanted to tell him how I felt, face to face.

* * *

I went on a Saturday. It took me four hours to get to Bellingham on the bus, and after the one change at the station in Seattle, it was mostly miles and miles of frozen forest. I had called the day before and talked to Paulo, and I'd asked him to tell George I'd be there. I figured George would decide for himself what to do.

On my lap I had my parka and my backpack. There was a blue ink stain on the pocket of my sweatshirt where a pen had leaked, which sort of matched my jeans, and in the pocket I had pinned the string with George's sailing knots. It had broken from wear over the summer but I'd kept it, and now I had it with me for good luck. I also had a book for class but it turned out I couldn't read much because my eyes were full of the landscape and my heart was full of the things I wanted to say and I didn't know if George would want to talk to me or even really be there. I might arrive and no one would be home, despite what Paulo said. George didn't owe me a thing.

* * *

I got to Bellingham around noon and found the house with a map a guy at the bus station drew for me on the back of an envelope. It wasn't too far. My heart was beating so hard when I got up to the door I could barely lift my hand to knock. Paulo answered and it was all kind of awkward, but he smiled and invited me to sit down and said George had just gone to drop off some paperwork for a client but would be back in about fifteen.

He said, "Want a cup of tea?"

"That would be great." I took off my parka and put it on top of my backpack on the floor. "I've never been up here before."

Paulo was just a few yards away in the kitchen running water into the kettle. "What do you think so far?"

"It seems pretty nice."

"Yeah, it's nicer in the summer."

Paulo and I didn't say anything for a few minutes. He was clinking cups and opening cabinets and I looked around their place. I didn't see anything of George's I recognized. I'd been worried I would see a photo of him with his new girlfriend or something like that, but I didn't. Then Paulo brought over the tea and holding the cup felt good on my hands.

I said, "How's your business going?"

"We're getting organized." He smiled. "It's a lot more paperwork than we expected. That's the un-fun part."

"For sure."

Then I heard the door.

My heart crushed into itself and George came in, and he kind of frowned and smiled at the same time, and he said, "You're really here."

The beard was gone and his hair was shorter, and he wasn't so tanned now. After so much time and seeing him so often in my mind it was a kind of a shock to see him in person. He sat down on the other end of the couch.

Paulo grabbed his coat and keys. "I have a few errands to do." He came over and gave me a hug and said it was nice to see me, and that gave me a little more courage to face George.

And after he left, George said, "Talia, why are you here?"

A massive lump formed in my throat and it took me a minute to be able to get any words out. George frowned at me like he was suspicious, but I just said, "I wanted to see you."

"Why? Why do you want to see me? What for? I need to know what for."

I'd never been so empty-handed in my life. I had nothing. Nothing other than the bare truth of what I wanted to say, but right that second it was all I needed.

I said, "Because I still love you."

The lump in my throat broke and tears started pouring down my cheeks. But I was solid too, rooted like a tree.

He stared at me.

For a second I couldn't move. I couldn't look away from his face, from his eyes. It felt like the whole past year was shooting through me, through my heart and stomach and arms and legs and up my spine.

George shook his head and his face kind of crumpled. He said, "If you came to tell me you want us to be friends..." he ran a hand over his forehead. "I can't be your friend. I can't. With you it's all or nothing. I've been friends with other exes, in the past, but I can't do that this time."

I wiped my eyes and my cheeks on my sleeve. "I don't want to be your friend."

I looked at the brown of his eyes, his black eyebrows. I knew the details of his face so well. I said, "I just needed to say it."

"Say what?"

"That I still love you. Even with everything that happened."

He shook his head again, "I don't understand what you want."

Time stopped, or my heart did.

"I want you."

He froze.

I said, "I want to be with you."

George pulled his eyes away and started pacing around the room. He ran his hands through his hair, and he whispered, "Shit..."

I stayed there sitting. All at once that feeling of solidity came over me again, stronger than ever. I was completely still inside. Tears were running down my cheeks again but inside I'd never felt so calm.

George stopped pacing and he knelt down in front of me. "Why now? Why are you saying this to me now?"

"I've been pretty confused. I mean, things have been confusing." I wiped my face again with my sleeve. I said, "I didn't know what was happening when you were away. I thought maybe you didn't actually care. I thought you might not actually come back." My voice was breaking now. The words were awful and wouldn't stack up right. I just wanted him to believe me. "I hurt you and I'm sorry. I messed up everything. I never wanted to hurt you."

George's eyes were wide. He looked down and covered his mouth with his hands a minute, then he said, "It's been a year almost, since I left."

"I know."

"I'm seeing someone."

"I know."

He came closer. He had tears in his eyes. "What do you expect me to do?"

I said, "I don't expect anything."

We sat there a long time without talking. His face was changing. He was looking at me like he used to, before he left, before I'd made us strangers.

He said, "I'm sorry I left. You can't take all the blame here."

I said, "I'm sorry I didn't wait, though."

He lifted his hand and touched my cheek. He smoothed my hair back and rubbed his thumb over the side of my jaw, and then we sat there looking at each other again a long time. I wanted to reach for him, but I didn't. He hadn't decided anything, and there was this other girl that he cared about, maybe he loved her. Maybe what we were doing right now was the good-bye.

And then, all at once I needed to step away. Being so close to him, and also not, was starting to hurt too much. I stood up. "Okay." I said, "I don't want to infringe on your life. I just wanted to talk face to face." I looked at the clock they had sitting on a table in the corner. "I'm going to go. I can catch the three o'clock bus."

George shook his head and ran his hand through his hair again, and he said, "I don't want you to go...but..." He stood up too. "You took me off guard, and I'm not processing right, I need to think things through." He blew out some air. "But let me walk you to the station."

* * *

When we were outside on the street, walking, George said, "How's school? Is it going alright?"

"Yeah, it's good." It was weird to talk about everyday things right then, but what else was there?

"Are you dancing?"

"A lot."

He nodded, started to say something else and then stopped himself.

I said, "Paulo said you guys were getting your business all organized."

He half-laughed. "We're getting there."

In a few minutes we were at the station. George looked up at the sign. I had to go in and I just had to hold myself together. It was still about half an hour until the bus would be leaving. I said, "I better wait by myself."

"Yeah, okay." He had his hands in his pockets and he looked pained.

I didn't know how we should say good-bye and I started to turn to go but he grabbed me, put his arms around me and we hugged. I gripped him hard, smelled his George smell, and then I pulled away.

* * *

I think I cried the whole way back to Olympia. I remembered Renee saying she thought the sky would run out of water, but I guessed now I understood because I never ran out of tears. Whatever mistakes I'd made, I'd have to live with the consequences, but it was more than that. The tears were washing me out, like rain.

I wanted to be with George. I wanted us to be together again and now I'd told him and that was all I could do. In one way, I was all torn up, but I also felt at peace. Sooner or later George would be in touch, when he was ready, or he wouldn't, and that would be his answer.

* * *

The next day I had work. It was Sunday, but I'd signed up to go in early to help with inventory, and when I left the house no one was up yet. I put a note by the phone saying I'd be at Media Loan in case anyone called.

The buses were almost empty and campus was very quiet and when I got to work Millie and Calvin were there with only a few others. Doing inventory was usually pretty tedious, but that day I was grateful for it. It was even kind of relaxing, listening to music and going through the shelves and bins of gear with long checklists, especially since I didn't think my brain could have dealt with any school work that day.

At lunch, I went with Millie and Calvin to the cafeteria and we got burritos and if I'd been in a different mood I'd have laughed at what passed for a burrito here in Washington, but I totally didn't care because it was food and that was all I needed. Millie asked me if anything was wrong, because I was so quiet, but I said I was okay, and then Calvin goes, "Something's really bothering you." I hadn't told him anything about going to Bellingham, but I guess by now he knew me pretty well.

Calvin had been very understanding about me breaking up with Toby. I was worried he might hold it against me since they were such good friends, but he'd said, "The heart is a complicated organ. I know that."

Now both he and Millie were looking at me. Millie kind of patted my shoulder with this very sweet look of concern.

Calvin said, "Do you want to talk about it?"

I shook my head. "Thanks for asking, though."

And then we just kept eating, and when we were done we got back to work, where a couple of times the phone rang but it was never for me.

* * *

It was dark by the time I got home. Renee and Hafsa were in the living room reading and I sat next to Renee on the couch. I asked if anyone had called and she said no. And then she said they had made soup if I wanted any and I said that would be great, thanks, and then I ate and went to bed early. Lying in the dark I thought how if going forward my life didn't include George, that eventually I'd let go and eventually I'd love someone else. I'd learned enough by now to know that, but it wasn't the life I wanted.

* * *

The next day was Monday and we all had class and work, and when I got home that evening there was still no message from George, and I started to think maybe it was foolish of me to go up to Bellingham like I did.

I didn't want to talk with Renee or Hafsa or even call Amy. Great friends though they were, I was afraid they would just tell me I should let it go, or screw him, or get over it, that it had been almost a year and I should have moved on, that he was the one who left and that things had run their course. I took my backpack up to my room. I felt so heavy going up the stairs, I didn't think I'd even be able to read, so I lay down on the bed and put on some music.

And while I was lying there I tried to think what Hari would say. I thought he would say that going to Bellingham and talking to George was the right thing to do because the decision came out of feeling connected to my intuition. He would say that when you stayed connected, one way or another the right thing would happen next. I kept thinking that no matter what happened, I did my part, and that Hari would understand.

And then there was a knock at my door.

"Come in."

Renee poked her head inside. She said, "George is downstairs."

* * *

He was there, standing by the door with his coat on. "Can you come out for a walk?"

My heart was like a wild animal in my chest. I didn't even answer, I just grabbed my coat and shoes and we stepped outside. His truck was parked in front of the house and we walked past it and crossed the street into the park and we walked around the whole block not saying anything. I knew by how George was breathing that he was getting ready to. Just the fact that he was there gave me so much hope, but I didn't know what was coming, and more than anything I wished I had a railing to hold onto.

Finally, we sat on the swings, and George cleared his throat. "Look, I talked to Sherry and I've been thinking about everything nonstop." And then he said, "And I've been thinking about what a chicken shit I've been."

I said, "Don't say that."

But he was angry. He said, "No, it's true. And I've been thinking how brave it was of you to come up and see me on Saturday. Just to come up to Bellingham by yourself and say what you did." He was crying, just a little. "And I don't see why I deserve someone like you."

He rubbed at his eyes with one hand. "I want you to know that I didn't expect you to wait, when I was in Mexico. I mean, I practically told you not to." He pinched the bridge of his nose, struggling. "That's why I left, partly."

This wasn't what I had expected him to say and I didn't understand. "What do you mean, why you left?"

He said, "Because you're so young. And I was falling for you so hard. It scared me." He took a big breath, like he was coming up from underwater. "All that time I was away I told myself it was for my career, for my future and all that."

"That's true though," I said. "Wasn't that true?"

"Yes and no. Yes, but also no." He said, "I was running."

My whole sense of what had happened began cracking into pieces, and the pieces started rearranging. I was beginning to see a new picture. Maybe it wasn't solely my fault after all. Maybe we'd both made things happen the way they did.

George's voice came out hoarse. "And I've been pushing my feelings for you away." He pinched the bridge of his nose again. "I shouldn't have let you take the bus home. I should have at least driven you home. I felt like such an asshole." He shook his head. "There are so many things I should have done or shouldn't have done."

My heart was beating against my ribs, against my lungs. I was desperate to know where this was headed. One more second would be too long.

I said, "It doesn't matter now. All that's in the past, and we're sitting here right now, so please tell me what else you came to say. You said you talked to your girlfriend. Tell me what you said."

He looked at me. "I said I had to stop seeing her. I told her about me and you, and I told her I needed to see you."

I couldn't breathe. I couldn't move. I was afraid I'd heard wrong, but finally I said, "You'll give us another chance?" My voice was shaking.

He reached for me, put his arms around my shoulders, and it was so awkward because of the swings that when I threw my arms around his neck we just fell out onto the cold wet sand. But that was the last thing in the world I would have cared about.

* * *

We went inside and up to my room and lay on the bed in the dark. I touched his face and he smoothed my hair back, and then I moved forward and kissed him, just lightly on the lips.

He whispered, "I've missed you so much, all this time."

I kissed him again and he held the back of my neck and I fumbled for the buttons on his shirt with my fingers and I kissed his collar bone. And little by little we undressed, and even though it had been almost a year since the last time, I remembered him completely, and when he pushed inside me love and pain merged together and it was everything I wanted. And because my arms were wrapped around him I felt his shoulders shaking, and for a second he just sobbed. I touched his tears with my thumb and I kissed his cheeks, and then he found my mouth and we started moving again, moving together, me and George.

21

We slept for a few hours, and then George had to leave at five in the morning. He and Paulo had work and he had to get back. He said Paulo had been dying to get out of Bellingham, and the truth was he was too and he didn't see why they couldn't move their business down to Olympia. Then he laughed, "Not to get ahead of myself."

I went outside with him to the truck and we kissed one last time through the window and he said he'd be back that night. When he drove away there still wasn't any light in the sky, not even one pale edge, but it was like the brightest, newest day.

* * *

He did come back and we stayed up late because there was so much catching up to do. We were getting to know each other again and we had to kiss for hours and hours. He said Paulo could do without him the next day so I skipped class and we spent half the day in bed and the rest of it just walking around and talking.

George told me everything about Mexico that he hadn't in his letters, which was a lot because we'd had so many gaps and now I could ask him questions. He said things to me in Spanish, including a handful of expressions he'd learned that were funny or poetic. I held his hand as we walked, and every now and then I lifted it up and I kissed it or I hugged it to my cheek or to my heart.

I showed George a bunch of comics I'd drawn over the summer based on things that had happened at work and at home with my new housemates, and he laughed reading them. He said the way I drew the people was the funniest part of it, and he wanted to know about school and all the stupid details of everything. He wanted to know about everything except for Toby. He didn't ask about that and I didn't tell him or want to, just like I didn't want to hear anything about the girl he had been seeing. Those were things we just left out.

George said he got to be really good friends with this one guy on the crew named Jaime and said he became like a second brother almost. He got a big envelope of photos out of his backpack, photos he'd taken down there, and later, after dinner, we went in my room and pored over them on the bed, and that led to a hundred more stories. There were several pictures of Jaime and he had this really sweet smile and George said that if his business with Paulo did well enough he'd invite Jaime to be a partner, because Jaime had told him he'd like to come north. George said that when he showed Jaime my picture, Jaime had made like he was stabbing himself in the heart and he'd said, "Beautiful."

George had a lot of pictures of the landscape too, and plants, and he showed me one of this big agave plant. He said that he especially liked the agaves and that there were so many different kinds, not just the kind they use to make tequila. And as he was talking that thing started happening, like when we used to watch movies, where in the middle I'd get interested in him instead, and this time it was his hands, his hands that I'd been holding all day.

I reached over and took his finger, the one that was pointing at an agave leaf and the pattern the spines had made on the adjacent leaf, and I made a fist around it and I pulled it toward me and I laid his hand against my face. And because I'd been lying on my side, I rolled onto my back and I slowly moved his hand down over my neck and over my chest and down to my waist, and by then he was leaning over me and we were kissing again and I pulled at his hips and we forgot about the photos for the rest of the night.

* * *

The next morning George left early, back up to Bellingham. We'd planned that I'd go up in a couple days for the weekend and I saw Renee in the kitchen and she said, "I see you've come up for air."

I said, "Yes, I have. For now."

She gave me a big kiss on the cheek. "You seem really happy." And then I started crying and she told me to stop or I was going to ruin her day.

It was weird, but when I got up to Bellingham I was almost as happy to see Paulo as I was to see George. Paulo came to the station in George's truck because, he told me, George had gotten temporarily tied up with something, and he gave me a big hug and lifted me way off my feet, which made me laugh like an idiot. He drove around to the harbor to show me their boat and then we went to their house, and by the time we got there George was back.

We hugged a long time and then sat on the couch, talking, and after a little while George said, "Hey, my mom invited us for dinner, is that okay?"

* * *

George and Paulo's mom lived on the second floor of an apartment building with a view of the water and she met us at the door wearing an apron with a frog on it. She was a petite lady, not as short as my mom but shorter than me and her name was Angela, and after she hugged and kissed George and Paulo she put her hands on my arms and kind of looked me up and down and said, "So this is Talia."

In the living room area, above a dark red couch, there was a big wall covered in framed family photos, several very old, with people looking formal and stern. Down below there were a bunch of George and Paulo as kids. I'd never seen pictures of George as a kid and I leaned close to those. George looked the same, but a kid version, with missing teeth and giant eyes and wearing goofy clothes from the seventies. And there was this one little black and white series of him when he was maybe thirteen or fourteen doing tricks on a skateboard, and he looked so young and lean and wild it kind of tore at me.

George goes, "Yeah, these are pretty embarrassing," and I just turned and hugged him.

I looked around at Angela's other things, like the sewing machine she had in one corner with a dressmaker's dummy standing next to it. I asked her if she sewed a lot and she said she did. She had a balcony crammed with planter boxes that she said she grew vegetables in during the summer, and she said the plants really grew because the balcony was south-facing and got a lot of light.

When it was time to eat, Angela had George and Paulo get the plates and everything, and she brought out a big pot of fish stew with a lot of tomatoes in it and we ate that with bread she sliced on a board on the table. George and Paulo dunked their bread in the stew and stuffed their faces and Angela just took her time eating. They looked a lot like her, Paulo especially, and they looked so big next to her. I wondered how two hyper guys like them ever came out of such a small, calm lady.

I asked Angela what she did for work and she said she was a legal secretary. I noticed she had a bit of an accent I hadn't heard before and she said she grew up near Cape Cod, in Massachusetts, and that she came out west when she was young, with the boys' dad.

After we ate, Angela rolled a thin little cigarette at the table and asked me if I minded tobacco and I said no, and while she was smoking it she asked all about my family and school.

She said, "So, what do you want to do in life?"

It was nerve-wracking, talking all about myself like that, especially about my future plans because I didn't have much of any, but she was nice and seemed interested.

I said, "I want to keep studying dance, maybe teach one day. And I'm also getting pretty focused on literature."

She nodded and tapped a little ash off onto her empty plate. "What kind?"

I said, "Probably American, but lately I've gotten interested in authors from India and Latin America."

She said, "George says you're very artistic."

I said, "I guess I draw a lot," and Paulo said she should commission me to do a family portrait. I thought he was joking, but she asked if I did pen and ink and I said I could.

While we were talking, George scooted his chair closer to mine and kind of played with my hair, and whenever I looked at him he just smiled.

* * *

When we said good night, Angela hugged and kissed George and Paulo again and told them to drive safe, even though they only lived about five minutes away, and she gave me a hug and kiss too and she said to George, "Well, she's as lovely as you said," and she kind of winked at me.

And later, when George and I were in bed, I said, "Your mom is so nice."

He said, "She really liked you. I knew she would."

"I really liked her too."

And then he started kissing me here and there and everywhere, and I put my arms around him and I thought how we probably weren't going to come up for air any time soon.

* * *

The next day I showed George part of the dance about Ganesh from Orissi class, and I told him what the movements meant, how it showed Ganesh's elephant ear and trunk and the other things, and when I was finished, George said, "It's beautiful. You're so beautiful doing it. I mean..." He held out his arms. He was sitting on the bed and I half-sat on his lap, and he held me and put his face against my neck and he said, "I'm just so glad you're here."

In the afternoon, we took a walk at the Western Washington campus, where back in the day George used to ride his skateboard from end to end. It was this long campus full of brick and big sculptures and while we were walking George told me how his smaller boat was finally almost finished, the one he'd been working on for ages, the one he took me out to see when we first met. He said he thought it would be done by April, by my birthday, and he wanted to take me out in it to celebrate.

I said I was going to be twenty, that I was almost twenty, and that I wouldn't be a teenager anymore and I asked him if I'd finally be old enough for him. He made a face like his friend Jaime did and pretended to stab himself in the heart. We'd been walking along this little wall by a big sculpture made of sheets of red metal. The clouds were breaking up and there were big patches of blue in the sky and the sun streaked in.

Suddenly, George took these two big, fast steps, and he jumped off the end of the wall into the air. The sun hit him, and just for a second he looked like he was flying.

PART FOUR

22

It was an early September evening, chilly outside but hot backstage and I was huddled up with the other dancers in the minutes before the start of our first performance. We were all decked out in full traditional costume--the garments, the jewelry, the ankle bells, the head pieces... We'd had a whole lesson just on how to do the make-up and how to paint designs on our hands and feet with a special red dye, and right then the heat and my nerves were making me lightheaded.

"Remember your breathing," Dr. Sundara told us in her high voice, standing straight as a lightning rod. "And to thank the Earth before you stomp on her."

The stage lights came up and the music started. We were on. My heart was beating too fast but my feet were making solid contact with the floor and right away I became submerged in the flow of the music and the beat of the drums.

The first dance was the one about Ganesh. By now it was as familiar and comfortable as an old friend, and somehow the strangeness of being on the stage drove me straight into the heart of it. I sensed the three personalities in the dance, Ganesh and his parents, Shiva and Parvati, coming through me stronger than they had before. I almost laughed when I danced as Ganesh, because he was jovial and lighthearted, with his big belly and elephant ears. He was graceful though, and precise and serious in his own way. Then with a turn and change in the hand gestures I was gentle Parvati, the mother doting over her child, and then powerful Shiva, fierce, with daggers of light shooting from his eyes. And this changed too when he became the proud father with his son on his knee. The faster part of the dance came last, making the ankle bells crash in a steady percussion, with rhythms in alternating patterns that spiraled into a grand conclusion, where we all froze in the last posture until the lights went down.

I was already sweating. My bracelets stuck to my wrists and a drop trickled down between my shoulder blades, but I felt vibrant and alive. We waited in the wings while another student group performed a music piece with a piano and two violins and then we went straight into the next dance.

This time I had to come out onto the stage in front of a big projection of the god Jagannath. The steps were agonizingly slow and high, and made my thigh muscles burn each time, and it was harder still because I had to turn and pivot on one foot with every step. I'd practiced my butt off for this one because the balance took such a long time to master, but what I didn't know was that the screen with the projection would be waving back and forth. I stepped and pivoted and faced the screen. It was only a couple of feet away and the waving suddenly threw off my balance, and for a second I panicked, thinking I was going to keel over, right there in the middle of the stage. I teetered backward, pressing my heel hard into the floor to try to regain my balance. But at the last moment I fixed my eyes on a faint line on the floor, and I made it. I smiled, despite myself. Jagannath had almost beat me, but I had won.

The last dance was my favorite. We all came out in the dark to the front of the stage and one by one we each picked up two little brass plates holding short, burning candles. When Dr. Sundara had first demonstrated the movement technique with the plates it looked like actual magic to me, because what she was doing seemed impossible. She raised and lowered the plates on her flat palms in these beautiful spirals, rotating her wrists and arms up over her head and back down again to the slow beat of the footwork. Doing the dance now by candle light enhanced effect and I heard the audience gasp, but I tried my best to ignore it. Any break in my focus and my plates would go down, as had happened many times in rehearsal.

Something a little bit magical happened for me too though, because as soon as I picked up my plates the whole notion of the technique kind of disappeared and in its place my hands and arms moved almost by themselves. My spine echoed the curves of the movements in a way I hadn't before, and this made my hips and shoulders move more freely. The music swept through my body like waves in the ocean, a force that bent my limbs into the right shapes. In my periphery the other dancers moved around with their plates, all those dancing flames, and at the center of it all I felt that quiet stillness, a presence, a different kind of ocean.

And then it was over.

All of us dancers, musicians, singers stepped out together to take our bows. The audience was applauding like mad, visible now that the house lights were up. I looked in the crowd for my friends and couldn't find them, until all of a sudden there they were, just a few rows back on one side. Renee was whistling with her fingers and Paulo was yelling something and I burst out laughing.

When we were free to go mingle with the audience I jumped down the stairs and made my way over to them. Paulo gave me a hug and told me I looked like a goddess, which made my face feel even hotter, and Renee and Hafsa said they loved it, though Renee said she was worried when I almost stepped off the edge of the stage. I hadn't even noticed that.

George's face was flushed and his eyes looked wet. He kind of blinked and shook his head, half-laughing. He took my hand and said, "I don't know what to say." He'd seen me practice, but he'd never seen the costumes or the entire dances, so I'd hoped it would still be surprising for him. I was about to ask him if he liked the show though, but both Paulo and Hafsa started to say good-bye, and then I spotted Toby and his girlfriend Camille over on the other side of the theater.

I had wondered if I'd see Toby there, because a couple of his friends had performed in the concert. It had been about a year now since we'd broken up. At first, I'd made a point to avoid running into him around campus and I was pretty sure he did the same. He knew my work schedule and he started picking up the equipment he needed when I wasn't there. Then, after the winter break, we crossed paths a couple of times and actually said hello, though it was brief and neither of us cracked a smile. Not long after that I started seeing him around with Camille and things shifted. He came into Media Loan a couple of times and it was friendlier, which was a big relief to me. I didn't think Toby and I would be hang-out friends, but I really wanted to be *some* kind of friends, and I knew Camille from a class and she was always pretty nice to me.

Now, though, a wave of prickly heat washed over me. I'd never been in a room with Toby and George at the same time and they had never met, and when I spotted Toby heading in my direction I had the sudden urge to flee. But instead I dug my toes into the nubbly carpet and gripped George's hand tighter.

And then Toby was right there, with Camille just behind him. He gave me a little side hug and said, "That was wicked."

I laughed, and Camille said, "You're a great dancer."

"Thanks, you guys," my face was really burning now.

I glanced at George but I couldn't read his expression, and when I introduced everyone Toby put out his hand, "Hey, George."

And George goes, "Hey, man." They shook hands, which was very surreal, and George told Camille it was nice to meet her. But then he turned around and walked over to one of the side doors that was open to the outside and he leaned against the frame. Renee gave me a look.

I just said, "I think he's getting some air." I would have liked a breath of fresh air myself. I thought my face was going to melt off, and my stomach wasn't feeling so good either. We stood there chatting another minute or two and then they left to go talk to Toby's friends.

I went backstage to get changed and everyone was pretty giddy. There'd been a few mistakes here and there, but we'd made it. Dr. Sundara came to tell us we did alright, then her husband chimed in and said we were great. He teased her for being too hard-pressed to give praise, and when we all said good-bye we did a bunch of little group hugs all around. I was cooling off now. I was glad, in a way, that George and Toby had finally met. I'd thought it would happen eventually and I was relieved to get it over with, but I didn't know what was up with George now and it made me uneasy.

When we drove home in the truck with Renee, George was pretty quiet. Renee and I talked about the performance and the other pieces and when we got to the house Renee got out but George didn't open his door. Renee gave me another look and said she'd see us inside. I just nodded.

I'd been squished up in the middle and I moved over. I looked at George. "Did I do anything wrong?"

He said, "So that was Toby, huh?"

"Yeah."

He didn't say anything for a minute, but then he said, "I think I might not stay over tonight. I don't think I'll be good company."

I felt my heart fall, "Okay."

He hadn't answered my question, and I still wondered if I had done something wrong or if he just thought I had. He seemed so far away and he wouldn't look at me, and in a way it reminded me of the time I'd gone to see him right after he came back from Mexico, and that scared the shit out of me.

I didn't want to say good night with that kind of distance hanging there between us, so I said, "Can we talk tomorrow?"

"For sure."

* * *

When I went inside, Renee was heating up water for tea. "Did George leave?"

"Yeah, he got weirded out meeting Toby." I'd been so happy right after the performance and now I was crushed. I sat down on the bench by the kitchen table. "Should I not have introduced them?"

Renee looped the string of a tea bag around the handle of a mug. "No, it would have been weirder not to." She poured the steaming water. "Do you want?"

I said no thanks, I was really tired all of sudden.

* * *

Lying in bed I thought about how far George and I had come. Those first few months when we were back together, early in the spring, George and Paulo were busy relocating their business and we were still living in separate cities. We did a lot of traveling to see each other, me to Bellingham and George to Olympia. I got used to reading on the bus and, more than that, George and I started getting used to each other again. We were the same people, but we were also different, and though we were getting closer all the time we were both a little haunted by the past.

The last time I was in Bellingham with George he got a letter from his friend Jaime in Mexico who was still working on the same boat. I had been doing stretches on the rug while he read the letter. "Jaime says there's work available if I want to come down."

And I guess it was how he said it, because my stomach all but fell out of my body. My heart started pounding, and when George saw my face and he said, "Hey, what's up?"

I just shook my head. He came over and sat next to me. "I'm not going or anything." I shrugged my shoulders. I thought if I said anything I might start crying. He said, "No, no. Of course I'm not going. That's not what I meant." He put his arms around me and kissed my head through my hair. "I'm not going to leave again."

I leaned into his shoulder. I took a few breaths and steadied myself. "You sure?"

"Completely."

* * *

The night after the performance I went over to George and Paulo's new place. Paulo was out and it was cold so George made a fire in their fireplace and we sat on the rug in front of it, throwing little twigs into the flames. He was more relaxed than the night before, but I was still nervous to bring up the subject so I just asked him how he was doing and he said, "Better."

He got the iron crow bar they used for a poker and rearranged one of the logs.

He said, "Yeah, last night took me by surprise." He was quiet another couple of minutes, then he said, "When I got that letter from you, about him, it was like I'd been waiting for it, like I'd been preparing myself, but then when it came I wasn't ready at all."

I moved closer to him and took his hand.

"That letter hit me like a truck."

"I'm sorry."

"No, you don't need to be sorry." He rubbed his thumb on the back of my hand. "We've been all through that. It's just that things out of the blue, like last night… It's like a vortex. I have to sort of retreat for a while until I get a handle on it."

"I get that." I was feeling relieved now, talking was a thousand times better than not talking.

He smiled a little, "Sorry I'm not Mr. Easygoing."

"Are you supposed to be?"

He half-laughed. "Maybe."

I laced my fingers in his.

He said, "I used to need to retreat a lot more, it was a real issue with me and Valerie." Valerie was his ex that he was with the longest, three years. He said they argued about it a lot by the end, and it made everything so much worse.

We didn't say anything for a while again, but then I really wanted to know what he'd thought of the show. I'd worked so hard for my first performance, and Orissi had been so important to me, one of the most vital things I'd ever done in my life.

I said, "So, did you like the show last night?"

George looked at me like he was caught by surprise again, but he said, "I loved it."

"Did you?"

"Oh, my God, yes, of course I did. It blew my mind."

I laughed.

He looked at the fire again. "There's something different about you when you dance. I was trying to put my finger on it last night. I don't know, it's almost like your soul shines out."

I laughed again, "Oh man."

He said, "But don't you feel like that?"

"Maybe a little."

He could see how I felt when I was dancing. He smiled with that crinkle at the corners of his eyes and I loved him so much it hurt. I pretended to stab myself in the heart and he laughed.

I threw a few more twigs into the fire. "I think Orissi has been growing me in all kinds of ways."

George stretched out on his side. "Like how?"

"Like it's feminine and strong at the same time. Usually feminine equals weak."

"I've never seen you as weak."

"Not just me personally, I guess, but being female I've always wanted better models than what I usually see. So Orissi gives me something that I've never found anywhere else." I said, "I feel like it lets me be more womanly. I don't know. Maybe that sounds silly..."

George rubbed my leg. "That's not silly at all."

23

Hafsa came by my room one night with a book she'd been reading. She tossed it on my bed. "You should read this."

"Should I?" I picked it up. It had a green cover with drawings of vines around the edges, like a book of fairy tales. *The Natural Woman*. "What's it about?"

"Natural birth control. You like natural stuff." I did like natural stuff. Hafsa was always teasing me about washing my hair with Dr. Bronner's and using cloth menstrual pads.

"Is it like the rhythm method?" I'd heard of that.

"Related, but no." She said it was a method called "observing your fertility," how you follow the physical signs of your body to know which days you aren't fertile, so you can have sex without other birth control. That sounded pretty interesting.

I didn't mind condoms, but the idea of not using them was exciting. I'd never wanted to go on the Pill though, too unnatural for me, and I didn't like the idea of a diaphragm either, what with all the spermicide you have to put up in there. I put my book on the history of India aside and started reading *The Natural Woman*. I ended up reading most of it that night. I'd never realized you could actually read your body's signs and use them that way, so the whole next month I tried observing myself. It didn't seem too hard. I got a pretty good idea of when my fertile time was, and the non-fertile days afterward that the book called the "Safe Zone."

When I asked George if he wanted to try it out, he said, "Are you sure about it?"

I said, "It's science."

He smiled and reached for me. "As long as you're sure, I'm game."

I laughed, "Wow, you're such a good sport."

He laughed too, "I'm a team player."

* * *

Several nights later we were sitting on my bed and I turned the light off. George moved my hair back and kissed my neck.

He said, "Are you ready for this?" I said I was and he said, "How do you feel?"

"Nervous, I guess." It was nerve-wracking removing the safety net. It was more of a mental leap than I'd expected, since I was letting go of a strict rule I'd had for myself. Rules were anchors, and without them I might drift too far, I might go right over the edge and never find my way back.

Not everyone was the stickler that I was about these things, I knew that. Calvin was, but I had friends that were pretty lackadaisical about protection, and that worried me. I'd kept that tight rein on myself because I knew how easy it would be to mess up. What if condomless sex turned me lackadaisical too?

George said, "Let's just kiss." And we did, but there was a charge in the air of trying this new thing and it made the kissing more potent, and before long we were both breathing harder. Finally, I couldn't take the suspense. I pulled his shirt off and he helped me off with mine and when we were undressed George moved on top of me and I slid my legs around him. He was hot and hard against my stomach, and then I felt the soft tip of it touch me where I was wet. Then he was in, skin touching skin with no barrier, and I shivered like it was our first time.

Where condoms always had a slightly squeaky-balloon quality, feeling George like this was almost velvety, and the sensation rippled into my belly. We went for a minute or two and I kept shivering, but then all of a sudden he pulled out, and blew a long breath with his head down. I said, "What's wrong?"

"Nothing. I just need to cool it for a second."

But he knew I didn't want to stop so he moved down and put his mouth on me. And then we were going at it again, and he gave this big push and before I knew it I was coming already, and then he did too, with a low, growling sound I hadn't heard him make before.

I put my mouth to his ear. "You're a wild animal."

"I'm a what?" He was catching his breath.

"A wild animal."

He laughed. "Just wildly in love with you, that's all."

Neither of us was sleepy yet so we lay there talking, until he started kissing my shoulder. He was pressed against my thigh and getting hard again and I felt a hot rush go through me. I pushed him onto his back and straddled him. He rubbed my thighs and he made his voice low like Barry White, like he sometimes did when he was being funny, and goes "Oh, yeah…"

I leaned down, "Shhh…" and I kissed him on the mouth and he held my hips with his strong hands and we rocked and rocked, turning all that heat into pure electricity.

* * *

But at times what was electric between us also created a shock. One evening after I was done on campus, I took the bus to George's house. When I got there he'd just pulled his truck into the driveway, and when he saw me didn't say hi right away. He was busy getting out his tool belt and other stuff and he had a dark-looking frown on his face.

He set his drill box on the ground and I picked it up to help take it inside. "You okay?"

He slammed the truck door closed. "Argument at work." He said a guy at his jobsite kept making stupid mistakes, dangerous ones, and was being a dick about it. George said it wouldn't matter that much, but he still had to work with the guy for the next few days.

"That sucks."

We carried all his stuff in, and when we put everything down in the entryway he gave me a hug. "Thanks." He rubbed his hair and bits of saw dust fell out. "I'm going to take a quick shower."

"Want a back rub later?"

He was already halfway down the hall. "Maybe."

I went to the kitchen to see what I could make for dinner. George worked hard and I knew he'd be pretty hungry, and I thought it would make him feel better if he could sit down and eat sooner than later. While I was rummaging around in the fridge Paulo came home from his job at the bike shop. During the off season, he and George still both had other jobs, which kept them from driving each other crazy. Living and working together could be a bit much.

Paulo had this little trick he did of riding his bike up the three front steps and bumping the door open with his front tire and then riding through the entryway, and when he came in the kitchen he said, "Hey, are you cooking?"

"I think so." I was finding random vegetables and figured I'd make a stir fry and rice.

Paulo started washing bike chain grease off his hands with a cleanser at the sink. "There's fish I can broil."

"That sounds good." I had no idea how to cook fish.

He got a beer from the fridge and hopped up on the counter. "How's dancing? Still in love with it?"

I smiled. "Yes."

I told him that I had been working on this one sequence with my practice group all afternoon that was really challenging, and he goes, "Can you show it to me?"

I gave the vegetables a stir in the pan and did my best to show him the steps. Paulo watched, nodding, and then said, "That doesn't look too hard." He got down from the counter and did this very hilarious rendition of the sequence and while I was in the middle of laughing my head off George came in half-dressed and rubbing his hair with a towel.

Paulo said, "Talia's teaching me some Orissi."

I said, "He's a natural." George's mood had put me on edge and I appreciated Paulo's comic relief.

Paulo did his dance again and George rolled his eyes, but to me it was even funnier. Then George left to finish getting dressed while Paulo danced more of his Orissi, and when I tried to make him bend his knees more, he grabbed me and threw me over his shoulder in a fireman's carry.

I tried to shout, "Hey!" but I was laughing too hard. George came in before I was back on my feet but I could see he was still frowning.

George was pretty quiet while we were eating and Paulo kept cracking jokes, which he tended to do when George got moody. Then Paulo took off to go see his new girlfriend, this girl Suzanne he'd met at the bike shop, and George and I started cleaning up. I was filling one side of the sink with soapy water and piling the dishes in when I reached in and accidentally grabbed an empty can that Paulo had left out. It sliced my finger pretty badly.

I pulled my hand out, "Shit!"

George goes, "What did you do?"

I put my finger under the running water. "Grabbed that can."

"You shouldn't put sharp things in soapy water."

"I know."

"You can't see them in there, that's really stupid."

"It was an accident."

He yanked the plug out of the sink, hell of exasperated, and grabbed my wrist. "Come on." He dragged me down the hall to the bathroom and started rifling through the cabinets for Band-Aids.

I held my finger over the sink, it was still bleeding a lot. "Why are you making such a big deal out of it? It was an accident."

"You should know better." He pulled down a bottle of hydrogen peroxide. "And if you don't clean it right it'll get infected."

"Jesus, I know that. Quit being so condescending, I'm not a toddler."

"Then don't act like one."

"What?" Maybe I was still sensitive about being younger, but that stung. I said, "You don't even care about this, you're just taking your stupid work stress out on me." When he didn't answer, I said, "I can do it myself."

"Fine." He banged out the door and down the hall. I heard water running in the kitchen. I stuck a few Band-Aids around my finger and then went in his room. I didn't want to follow him into the kitchen but I was too mad to sit still. I started pacing around. I'd been trying to be extra nice to George by making dinner and everything, and now he was being an asshole. It wasn't my fault he'd been stuck working with that stupid guy. I picked up one of George's pillows and threw it across the room. Then I started jumping on the bed.

He didn't have a futon anymore, it was a mattress with springs and it was pretty bouncy and I jumped as hard as I could, almost hitting my head on the ceiling. Now I really was acting like a toddler but I didn't care.

The covers got all messed up and the sheets came off the corners and then the bedframe started clacking against the wall.

George came in and stared at me. "What the fuck are you doing?"

"I'm jumping on the fucking bed!"

"Oh, shit." He left again and I went right on jumping.

Finally, I got tired and sat down. The bed was a total mess, the mattress half off the box spring and the covers on the floor. My finger was throbbing and I just sat there panting.

A few minutes later George came back again. He looked at me and looked at the shambles of the bed, and he said, "Jesus. I can't take you anywhere."

I didn't want to laugh or smile, but annoyingly I couldn't help it, and then neither could he. He sighed. "I'll try to contain my work stress. You're right that it's affecting me." He sat down next to me. "I do care about your stupid finger though."

I said, "Me and my stupid finger," and that made us laugh a little more. I hung out with him in the kitchen while he finished washing the dishes, and then he helped me fix the bed, but before long we were messing it up again.

24

Things were still off though. George's work had improved once he wasn't working with the one guy anymore, but he wasn't quite his usual self. For the next couple of weeks I'd feel thrown by even subtle things that would happen between us, like a look on his face or a tone in his voice, anything that looked like evidence of annoyance or distance. I thought I was probably making too much of it all, but there was this ping-ponging effect that kept me spinning. Thankfully, anytime I was over at his house and Paulo was there he put me at ease by being extra chummy. He'd notice George's mood and go, "Don't mind my brother," or he'd lean in and whisper, "He's a werewolf. And it's almost the full moon." He even called George "The Wolfman." Like, "Hey, Wolfman, do you have any quarters? I need to do laundry."

If I tried to ask George if anything was wrong, he'd say, "No, there's isn't. Really. I promise." So, after a while I just left it alone.

* * *

Just after Thanksgiving it snowed and overnight the temperature dropped so low our pipes froze. One of them broke in the ceiling over Renee's bedroom, and while the landlord was fixing it I gave her my room and stayed at George's for a few days. Then in the middle of the second night I ran into Paulo in the hallway.

I was half-asleep, stumbling in the dark toward the bathroom, and when I went around the little corner he was suddenly right there, his hair tousled and no shirt on, and I was so startled I whispered, "Oh shit!"

He grabbed my hand, and goes, "Hey."

His voice was sleepy and the contours of his chest were visible in the light filtering in from the snow outside the bathroom window and for that split second we were so close I even smelled him. All I had on was an oversized t-shirt, I was almost naked, and I felt a pulse from his hand, a little bloom of attraction between us and this scared me a lot more than bumping into him in the dark.

I squeaked out, "Sorry!" and hopped into the bathroom.

I stayed in there longer than necessary. I knew Paulo was a handsome guy, I'd seen the way women looked at him, but I'd never looked at him like that. I was supposed to be in love with his brother, so what the hell was wrong with me? When I finally poked my head out the bathroom door there was no sign of Paulo. I tiptoed down the hall and got back in bed. George turned over and hugged me in his sleep, and I curled up around his arm with my stomach in a twisted knot.

It took me a while to get back to sleep, but when I did I dreamed that somehow I'd ended up in bed with Paulo and done the unforgivable, and George had found out. In the dream I was crying and begging George not to leave, sobbing that it had all been a mistake, but he wouldn't answer me and I knew I'd never see him again.

I woke up with my heart pounding. It was still dark and George was snoring softly, innocent of the crime, and when I realized it was all a dream I almost cried with relief. But I was still pretty confused. I wasn't attracted to Paulo, or at least I never thought I was. A scene appeared in my mind, like in one of those old-timey cowboy movies, where the man gets killed and then the woman marries his brother, because I did have a kind of love for Paulo, but I had always thought it was the sisterly kind. And then I thought, *Why am I thinking this?*

The part that scared me the most was feeling how close the line of destruction was. Like, if you stand on the edge of a cliff or you're driving on a busy highway, and you see how with one step or a yank on the wheel death would be right there. Or five minutes half-dressed in a dark hallway, and it's all over. I realized that there weren't any walls built around relationships, no safety nets. All George and I had were the decisions we made, countless little decisions that added up to what we had together. One swerve away and it would all come crashing down. Maybe it was nothing more than a free fall.

* * *

A couple of nights later I was at home in the kitchen with Renee and Hafsa and I told them about the hallway moment with Paulo.

Renee was standing at the stove stirring a pot of soup. She looked at me over her shoulder. "Are you worried about it?"

I said, "I mean, not really, but I don't understand it."

Hafsa was sitting on the bench, eating a bowl of ramen noodles with chopsticks. "Hormones. Nothing to understand."

"You think?"

"I mean, if you're committed to George--"

"I am, I am."

"And you don't have actual feelings for Paulo--"

"No!" I was sure I didn't.

"Then don't worry."

Renee nodded, "She's right."

Hafsa said, "This stuff just happens."

"Why, though?"

Hafsa looked me up and down, squinting. "Are you ovulating around now?"

I thought about it. "Actually, yeah."

"That's it then. Hormones, like I said. They can get overboard when you're fertile, the river can overrun its banks."

Renee laughed, "How poetic."

"What about for guys, though?" I said. "They're fertile all the time."

Renee gave me a look like the answer was obvious.

I didn't really want to think about George desiring other women but I figured it had to happen. "Aagh," I pulled at the collar of my shirt. It was feeling too tight right then.

Then Renee goes, "Seriously though, how are you *not* going to have at least a little crush on Paulo? That boy is *hot*."

I laughed. She was right. I said, "You should see him with his shirt off."

And Hafsa goes, "I'd faint." She looked dreamily into the air. "Mmm..."

We all laughed and it didn't seem so bad anymore.

* * *

But before long I got tripped up again. One day after dance practice I managed to just catch the bus before it pulled away. I flashed my pass at the driver and the first empty seat I found was right next to Toby.

He was listening to music on his headphones and reading at the same time. I never understood how he could do that. And he didn't see me until I was right there.

I said, "Can I sit?"

"Yeah, yeah." He smiled and moved his backpack from the seat onto his lap.

"Going home?"

"Just after I stop at the store. I'm out of pancake mix."

It was almost winter break and I asked him what he was doing. He said, "The usual," which meant going back to Spokane. "You?"

"The usual too."

Toby had his knees propped up on the seat in front of us, the cuffs of his pants were wet from the snow and I could hear the engine chugging under the floor. Outside the windows the gray of the sky was starting to darken and go blue. I remembered all those walks we took when we were first getting to know each other.

He said, "Hey, I was thinking about you the other day because I'm reading *Catch-22* for one of my classes."

"Really? What class?"

"Alternate Representations of World War II. We're reading *Slaughter House Five* next week."

"That's too fun for a reading list."

"I know."

Toby said his favorite character in *Catch-22* was Major Major Major Major, just because of the name. Then we got onto political satire and ways to use it in music, which was a new interest of his and the reason he'd signed up for that class.

Every time the bus swung around a corner we'd be momentarily pressed up against each other. A year ago, I would have laid my head on his shoulder or said something in his ear, but that was different now. We weren't a couple anymore and we were with other people, the decisions we'd both made were like a line between us. It was almost visible, a glowing thread, and like with Paulo in the hallway I became hyperaware of how easy it would be to cross that line, like if I grabbed his hand or his knee. Not that I wanted to, or that he would want me to, but the existence of the line and how easy it would take to cross it and the size of the ramifications became hypnotizing. It was like everything was *that* fragile.

When we got to downtown and were about to go our separate ways I wondered how we'd say good-bye. Our friend-relationship was still slowly developing and the talk and the ride made me feel close to him. Maybe that would translate into a good-bye hug. But with the dividing lines being what they were I just didn't know, so I stood there and I told him that it was really nice to see him, and he smiled. Then he put out his fist like I was supposed to bonk my fist on top of it, and so I did.

* * *

I walked around downtown a while, up to Sylvester Park and back. I was headed to George's but it was twilight and there was snow in little heaps around the bottoms of the streetlights and along the boulevards, and I didn't have to hurry. I kept thinking about the lines between people. Solid lines and dotted ones, and others that shifted and moved and were even elastic in a way that reminded me of playing loop jump rope when I was a kid.

But underneath all that was something truer. It was just love in its different forms. My heart was made to keep different kinds of love all at the same time, and there was nothing confusing to me about that. It was as clear as the sharp spike of ice in the air.

Later when I got to George's house I told him about seeing Toby and that we chatted on the bus. I told him because I wanted it to be the normal thing it was, though I was nervous he'd get upset, but he just said, "That's cool."

There was no vortex this time. George said being friendly with exes was always a good thing, if it worked out that way. He asked me about the rest of my day and what I felt like eating, and when he leaned over the sink to wash some carrots I grabbed him so hard around the waist he said, "Hey, what's up?" I didn't answer, I just stuck my head under his shirt and pressed my face to the warm skin of his back, and he laughed, "Talia the mole."

25

At the beginning of winter break Renee and I drove down again to California. Renee took the first leg of the drive, a couple of hours in the dark until the sun struggled to come up behind the frozen clouds. We shuffled through tapes like they were poker chips, bargaining between the Velvet Underground and Public Enemy, since even though there was overlap in our musical tastes we also definitely clashed.

Driving through Oregon we started talking about an exhibition in the library gallery Renee had been part of. She'd done a photo essay called "Weightless" on women swimming and Hafsa had agreed to be her subject, though the images were sort of abstract and you couldn't really tell it was her. Media Loan had two underwater cameras, big clunky things encased in yellow plastic, and Renee had used one of those to make the images of Hafsa, submerged in the water in mid-motion, in light and shadow and swirls of air bubbles. She gave me a few of the extra prints because I'd loved the images so much.

Later on Renee asked me if I'd thought about inviting George down to Ukiah and I said I had, and he wanted to but his mom was moving to a new apartment and both George and Paulo had promised to help her.

I said, "Maybe we'll go in the summer though."

"Really?"

"Yeah, visit his dad in Oregon on the way too."

She smiled. "Sounds hella serious."

"It would be so weird to have him in Ukiah," I said. "I'm not sure why he'd really want to go there."

"Meet the forces of nature that begat you."

I laughed. "Forces of nature."

I rolled down the window. I was chewing gum and I wanted to spit it out. For a second the freezing wind whipped my face and Renee said something that I didn't quite hear. When I turned back she was fiddling with the tape deck.

I rolled the window back up. "What did you say?"

"I said, he'll want to see the things that made you *you*."

* * *

I missed George a lot over the break. Not in the gut-wrenching way I had in harder times, but in an extremely restless way. One of the nights I was at my dad's the phone rang in its spot by the toaster in the kitchen. I was camped out reading in the hallway next to the gas heater and I heard my dad answer.

"Hello?... Yes, it is... Nice to meet you too... Not much, doing a lot of taking it easy... I'm sure it is..." My ears perked up. I was sure it was George on the line the way my dad kept chatting away, and my heart got fluttery. I wondered what kinds of questions George was asking him, what he thought of my dad's slightly stuttering, soft-spoken manner. The various pieces of my life had been so separate up to now.

My dad said, "Talia said you work with sailboats?" And then I imagined George talking about his work, painting a kind of preliminary picture of himself.

Finally, my dad said, "You too... I'll put her on." And to me, "It's Geo-orge."

I carried the phone, the long cord dragging over the worn-out carpet, into my old room and shut the door. And then George was in Ukiah with me after all. I lay down on the floor and stuck my feet up on the wall, balancing the heavy body of the phone on my stomach and pressing the clunky receiver to my ear. I'd been twelve years old when I first moved into that room. I decorated it with a lot of animal pictures and other cute things, and a year or two later the cute things came down to be replaced with things I thought were cool, and then when I was seventeen it all got packed up or given away, and now I was almost twenty-one.

George told me about helping his mom move to her new place and how she'd given him a few of his grandfather's old things he wanted to show me, like an ancient brass navigational tool called a sextant.

I laughed, "What a word."

"I know." He laughed too. "It's really cool though. I'm going to learn how to use it."

He said it wasn't the same there without me, that he missed me and couldn't wait to put his arms around me.

I said me too, and that I wanted to play with his sextant, and he laughed.

Afterward when I brought the phone back out, my dad said, "George seems like a nice person."

I smiled. "He is."

He broke into a hoarse, slightly off-key bit of song. "*Let the chips fall where they will... 'Cause I've got boats to build...*"

"Oh jeez. What's that?"

"An old country song. You could sing it to George." He chuckled.

I rolled my eyes. "Great idea."

* * *

On Christmas day George called me at my mom's and they had the same kind of chat, and after he and I talked, my mom said, "So what do you like about him?"

She was in the rocking chair peeling a bowl of garlic cloves with a paring knife and I sat on the red step stool next to the woodstove. She always made that kind of question sound like, "Why would you like a person like *that*?" and I didn't answer right away. I couldn't just tell her all the things I felt, be that personal. Like how I loved his voice and his touch and the way he got excited about things and how he could build anything out of wood, or how he loved me and understood me like no one ever had. So instead I said, "He's creative," which was true. And, "Good sense of humor," also true.

She rummaged around in the bowl. "Sounds like your speed."

I said, "Yeah, he's my speed." And we left it at that.

I hadn't been too focused on George meeting my parents. They'd met a lot of my friends over the years, but never a boyfriend and that seemed like a bigger deal, if only because it would reveal more about my private life. Plus, my parents weren't necessarily the regular sort and I thought it would be pretty awkward. But now it was like George had shown up on his own and presented himself to them, and once it had happened, on the phone at least, I was really touched he'd made the effort.

* * *

A few weeks after I got back to Olympia there was a party up at Marco and Anita's new place on the West Side. It was supposed to be musical, like all their parties, but bigger because it was a housewarming thing too, and George said they had news to share. I think he knew what it was already but he didn't say, and then in the middle of everything, Marco stood on a chair in the living room and started clinking a knife on a beer bottle.

When it quieted down, he thanked everyone for coming, and then he said, "And I hope you'll all come to the wedding in July." He was holding Anita's hand and he bent down and kissed it, and they were both smiling like mad and this giant cheer rose up around the room. George cupped his hands around his mouth and let out a big whoop. He shook his head, "They're really doing it," and he made his way through the throng to Marco and Anita and kind of pounced on them.

But then I noticed this woman go over to George and touch his elbow and when he saw her his mouth fell open. She was wearing jeans and a black sweater and she had light reddish-brown hair to her shoulders and her features were sort of delicate and pointy. She was quite pretty. I stepped closer and I heard him say, "Valerie," and then I knew it was his ex-girlfriend, the one he was with the longest. He'd told me she lived in Portland now, so I guessed she came up for the party.

George reached for my hand and tugged me over. "Hey, Talia, meet Valerie."

I got a tad queasy in my stomach, but I did my best to smile. "Hello."

She smiled back, warmly, and put out her hand. "So nice to meet you."

"You too."

She seemed so grown up compared to me, I guessed the same age as George and Marco and Anita. The only ex I'd met of George's was that girl Kayla, and Valerie was clearly in a different category.

While we were talking, I noticed that George was smiling his shy smile, like he used to when we first were getting to know each other, the one that made his eyes crinkle up in that certain way. It was noisy so he and Valerie had to put their heads close together to talk. She was smiling too, sort of intimately, and suddenly I sensed there was something going on that I wasn't a part of. It wasn't that I thought I should worry, but there was a vibe there and whatever it was I didn't think I could stand there and watch. I wasn't always Mr. Easygoing either.

I leaned over to George and said I was going to go say congratulations to Anita. He said okay, and just before I left he pulled my hand and gave me a little kiss on the mouth, which made me feel better to tell the truth.

George had told me about his relationship with Valerie and the things that caused their break up and I'd never gotten the feeling he still missed her or anything, but they were together for three years--a lot longer than he and I had been.

I found Anita and gave her a big hug. She had this wonderful radiant smile and for a minute I was kind of dazzled by it and I thought what a lucky guy Marco was. She was sitting with a clump of friends and her sister Racine, talking about wedding plans. Racine was just as beautiful as Anita. I hadn't met their other two sisters but I supposed they were all gorgeous, and I wished for the millionth time I had sisters too.

Anita said they weren't going to be doing anything super formal but they were hoping George would be their best man and I said I was sure he would. I looked back over to where George and Valerie were still talking. They weren't smiling like before but they were very focused on each other so I stayed with Anita, and I was fine sitting there, but I did kind of wonder how long George and Valerie would be holed up in the corner.

But the next time I looked over, they weren't there anymore. I started feeling twitchy. I got up and wandered around the house, squeezing past people who were drinking and laughing, jolly as could be. I told myself I wasn't looking for George, that I just needed to move around, but it was a lie. I thought maybe they'd gone in the kitchen to get a drink or something but they weren't in there, and they weren't in the entryway or the hall or on the stairs where a bunch of people were hanging out.

I even peeked in the bedrooms upstairs, where no one was, just a lot of coats piled up on the beds.

The longer I looked the more nervous I got. I didn't understand where they could be, it was so weird. Right then I had this image of the two of them making out in the bathroom, as if seeing each other had reignited the old passion, or maybe they had even left the party together. I knew it was totally crazy, but it scared me anyway.

Then I was in the living room again and passed by the front windows where one of the curtains was pulled to the side, and I caught sight of George and Valerie out on the porch, sitting on the stairs. All at once I was relieved because he hadn't left, but pretty unnerved because they were still alone together. I might have gone out there to say a friendly hello, but I was too busy feeling forgotten and like I didn't measure up to someone older and that pretty and who'd had such a big role in George's life.

I cut through toward the back of the house and went out the kitchen door. There was a slope in the back, and the back porch had a flight of narrow stairs that led down into the yard. I walked down there and stood on the grass. I could still hear voices and music from the party, muffled though, and an occasional car going by on the street. I watched the wind pushing at the black shapes of the treetops.

I was out there for a while. It was disturbing how much loneliness could come blowing straight out of nowhere. Then a slice of light fell out across the grass.

The back door had opened and I heard footsteps on the stairs.

"Talia," it was George. "What are you doing out here?" He tried to put his arm around me but I moved away. He said, "What's wrong?"

I shook my head at the ground. "Well, you were pretty busy. So."

"What, talking with Valerie you mean?"

I shrugged.

He said, "We were talking for a while, yeah. It was a good talk. We've both realized a lot of things since we broke up. You know."

I thought, *Like what? Like how you still have the hots for each other?* I clamped my mouth shut in time, thank God. But I did say, "Like what?" in a very demanding way.

"Like how we dealt with stuff. With each other. In the past. It was good to talk about it."

"Why did you go outside? Why did you need so much privacy all of a sudden?"

"Shit..." He ran a hand through his hair. I knew he was shocked by me being upset. "It was noisy inside, it was hard to hear."

I believed him, and it made sense, but I was still feeling twitchy all over and a lump had risen up in my throat. I kicked at the ground. "I thought maybe you'd left with her."

"Jesus, why would I leave with her? How could you think that?"

"I don't know." A few tears leaked out and I shoved them away with my wrist.

"I don't have feelings for Valerie, I love *you*."

"Okay." I still couldn't look at him.

He put his arms around me, but I kept mine at my sides. "Hug me."

"No."

He dropped his arms. "Fuck, Talia, we were just talking. I don't understand."

My throat was still all choked up and my voice wouldn't work. It was stuffed way down in my stomach somewhere. Finally, I said, "Vortex."

That talk we'd had about Toby. Vortex was George's word and I hoped he'd understand.

He was frozen a second, then he breathed out. "Vortex, huh?" He hugged me again and this time I leaned into him. "I love *you*, Talia. I'm with *you*. That's it."

I hugged him back. All that twitchiness and confusion started letting go.

* * *

We stayed at the party late into the night. Valerie left a couple hours before we did, and she and George did hug good-bye but it really seemed like nothing more than friendly. When there were just a few people left, Anita asked George about being their best man, and he said, "I'll be upset if I'm not."

Marco was half-asleep but he started smiling and gently beating George on the arm, and Anita said George would share the best man job with her sisters.

Later when we said goodnight, Anita said to me, "Let's have tea one day. Do you want to?"

I said, "For sure. I'd love that."

* * *

We'd never actually made plans, just the two of us, and we met the next Sunday at a café downtown. It was warmer than usual and finally dry so we decided to walk around by the harbor. After a while we sat on a bench by the water. The air smelled like seaweed and tar, but the wind was fresh, and I asked her what it was like to be engaged.

She said, "It feels really normal and really wild at the same time."

"Do you want kids and all that?"

She laughed. "Probably in a couple of years. I'm almost thirty so we don't want to wait too long." She was looking out at the water, but then she turned and looked at me very pointedly and I had this funny feeling like she was looking through my face and right into my mind.

She said, "You know, George is very special to me." She said he was one of the first people she met at the college, about ten years ago, and that they'd always been close. She said she'd seen him go through a lot of relationships.

Anita had her hair in two thick braids and the wind was blowing the shorter wisps around and she tucked them behind her ears. She said, "When he first met you, I could tell there was something different going on for him. He was really struck. And then when I met you I understood, because it was like you had a special quality that he did too, and there was this match."

It *was* like she was seeing into my mind, but seeing a question I didn't even know I had, and as she was talking I began feeling like a sun was rising in my chest. Honestly, I would have believed anything she said, she always seemed so wise to me, but this was especially meaningful because I wanted to believe I was important in George's life, as important as he was in mine, even if he'd been with a lot more people than I had, and for more time, like with Valerie.

Anita said that back then she was really happy for George, but she did have the same concern he did, about the difference in our ages and us being in different stages of life and because I was coming into it without much experience.

I shifted in my seat. "Almost none."

"Right. And then when he left for Mexico and things fell apart... It was really hard to watch that."

My sunrise feeling went cold. I wondered if she'd thought I was a terrible person, but I was too scared to ask. She noticed the look on my face though and reached over and gave my hand a squeeze. "But you guys made it through that." I nodded and wiped at my eyes, and she said, "So, I don't think I'm worried anymore."

I took a breath. "You don't think so?"

"Well, to be perfectly honest, that worry isn't completely gone."

I said, "Are you asking me what my intentions are?"

She laughed. "Maybe I am." She said she didn't expect me to be thinking in terms of forever, she herself wasn't really able to think that way until she was maybe twenty-five, but she'd still wanted to ask me about it.

I said, "I don't really know what to say, but I love him."

Everyone said you had to be with a lot of different people before you eventually settled down, that it was unhealthy if you didn't, and I was sure there was a lot of truth in that.

I said, "I know I'm young, but I've learned a lot in the last two years, because a lot has happened, and I can't imagine loving anyone more than I love George, or a relationship being better. I'm old enough to know there's always stuff you have to work on." Saying all this was making me tear up again.

Anita looked at me a while, and then she smiled. "That's good enough for me."

26

Soon after spring break we started having extra dance rehearsals and meetings with our practice groups because Dr. Sundara was getting us ready for a performance at a dance festival in Seattle. We had a lot of new material to learn, and I was so caught up in it that I didn't notice that the day on my calendar marked with a red P came and my period didn't. I didn't notice until two days later, and when the next two days came and went and I still hadn't gotten it, I started to feel uneasy.

I told Renee and she said, "Don't panic," and she asked me if it was ever late for no reason. I said it was late a couple of times, a long time ago, back when I had nothing to worry about, but I wasn't even completely sure because I hadn't kept track that closely. She looked uncertain, but she said again, "Don't panic. Just wait a few more days."

I said, "And then panic?"

"Probably."

The entire next day at school I kept ducking into the bathroom to check things out, but nothing. I had a dance practice in the afternoon with my group, and when we were taking a break one of the girls asked me if I was okay. She said, "You seem a little distracted," and I said I was just tired and a bit out of it. She looked at me like she didn't quite believe me, but she didn't pry.

An hour later we were finishing up and I spotted George out in the hallway. He was working at a jobsite nearby that day and was picking me up, and he was excited because he'd just gotten a contract to rebuild a sailboat for a guy he'd met at the boat yard. I didn't want to spring my worries on him right away so we talked about the sailboat job on the way to his house.

When we got to George's he got ready for a shower and I lay down on his bed. I was feeling tired after all and I even dozed off a tiny bit, and the next thing I knew George was sitting down next to me.

He rubbed his thumb over my forehead and then leaned down and kissed me on the cheek and he smiled and said, "I was hoping you'd get in the shower with me." I sat up and when I didn't smile back, he said, "You okay?"

I told him about being five days late and he kind of froze and his eyes got big, and he said, "Are you worried?"

"A little."

He nodded and bit his lip.

I asked him if this had ever happened with anyone else he was with and he said once or twice there was a concern but it never amounted to anything. He said, "What should we do?"

"There's nothing to do right now, just wait."

"You want to read while I make dinner?"

I said that would be great, because I was still tired. I put my face against his shoulder and he put his arms around me, still all warm and fresh from the shower, and he said, "Whatever you want to do, we'll do." And I didn't know if he was talking about now or the future, but it was comforting to hear him say it.

* * *

Two more days ticked by and there was no change, other than me feeling more anxious. I started going over and over the past month in my mind, the stages of my cycle and when George and I had sex without a condom and it all seemed in order, but maybe I'd missed something. I didn't write it all down in a diary or anything and I wondered if someplace I had miscalculated. When I was in bed I poked at my stomach. Nothing felt any different than normal, I wasn't having any unusual sensations, so I told myself not to worry, because if worse came to worse all I had to do was go to the clinic and get it taken care of, even though I'd heard it was no picnic to go through.

I knew a handful of people around school who were parents already, people my age, but I'd always thought I'd be much, much older before having a baby and so I'd always been extremely careful. But now it was killing me that I must have actually been careless about this horribly important thing. On the evening of the eighth day, Renee asked me how it was going and I said there was still nothing yet.

I said, "How could I have fucked up like this?"

And she goes, "Because maybe you're human?"

She said I was the most careful person she knew, but it could happen to anyone, and of course she was right. She said, "Are you going to take a pregnancy test? You can get one at the Health Center."

"I will if it comes to that." I'd read in *The Natural Woman* that you had to be two weeks late or more for a test to work.

* * *

Later when George came over and we were sitting on my bed talking, he said, "Do you know what you'd want to do about it?"

I said, "If I'm actually pregnant?"

He nodded, and then he brought my hand up and kissed my knuckles and he said, "Because I would support whatever you wanted to do."

"You would?"

He sort of jumped up and stuck his hands in his pockets and spun around, and he said, "Yeah, I mean like I'd support you either way," and I was so stunned I thought I'd have to sit down if I wasn't already.

George said, "Like if there was a baby, your baby... Our baby. I mean, if there was a baby." He ran his hands through his hair. "Jesus, it sounds crazy, but these things happen, and with you, I'd do it." He went down on his knees in front of me and took my hands and looked me in the eyes, and he said, "I just want you to know I'd be prepared to do that. Get married, whatever, take care of you." Then he looked down and half-laughed and said, "I mean, if you thought you could put up with me."

I said, "I wasn't really thinking about all that," and my voice kind of broke and I said I'd really have to give it some thought, and right then I felt like I might throw up and then I panicked, thinking that I truly was pregnant.

George said, "But it's up to you. It has to be up to you. And it still might be nothing at all, it still might..." but he didn't finish, because I was hugging a pillow and shaking like a leaf. And then we lay down, and he was holding me from behind and saying it was going to be okay, and I knew he was right, but I just kept shaking.

* * *

All the next day this feeling bothered me, like a little splinter under a nail. Just when I'd always assumed I knew what I'd do, I had to admit that I had this little doubt and I had to be honest with myself, and that meant considering the other option of actually keeping the baby. If there was one. Because what George said had really affected me, and it did seem crazy but if I had a doubt I had to face it, I knew I did, or else I might regret it the rest of my life. That theoretical third option, of having the baby and giving it up for adoption, wasn't a choice I personally could consider. I knew if I carried a baby to term and gave birth to it I would never give it up.

The whole day I thought about the people I knew at school who were parents, young parents with babies or toddlers, like the two guys from my work who both had families, and this one couple I knew from class who had their baby the year before, when they were both twenty.

Once, in the fall I was hanging out with them and their baby, a little boy, on Red Square, and they said they believed in starting a family young while they still had lots of energy. They were so comfortable with each other and the baby they made it look easy.

All of the young parents I knew still went to school and worked, it wasn't like anyone's life had ended, and the kids were all pretty cute. I thought about the daycare center on campus where one of my dance friends worked, and how there were more parents around than maybe I realized.

Just a couple of months ago even, this girl named Jade who was an advanced Orissi student the year before came to our class with her little baby in a sling. Dr. Sundara held the baby and said she would surely grow up to be a dancer like her mama, especially since she began her life dancing in the womb, because Jade was still dancing when she was pregnant. I thought how all my friends would probably think I was insane to even be thinking this way, and so would my parents. They'd probably be upset if they knew, especially my mom, even though they'd always pretty much let me do what I wanted and make my own decisions. They had their own lives and we never talked about stuff like this.

* * *

That night I had another one of my crazy dreams. I was at the marina with George and he wanted me to come onto his small boat. He said, "I want to show you something." We climbed down into the hold and he picked up a pile of blankets and when he turned around he was holding this baby with big brown eyes and wispy dark hair.

I said, "Whose baby is that?" It seemed like a boy baby, and I said, "Is he ours?"

And George goes, "I'm not sure, but I really love him."

Then I was holding the baby and I felt this overwhelming tenderness, but I still didn't know if he was ours or not, so I said, "We have to find out who he belongs to," and I was so worried about finding out that I started crying, and the next thing I knew George was shaking my shoulder.

He was hovering over me and we were in the bed and he was saying, "Talia.. Talia..." I reached out and hugged him, and he said, "I thought you were crying."

I thought I had been crying too but my eyes were dry and I knew I'd been dreaming, even though it hadn't totally faded away yet and I could still see the baby's face and feel that tenderness. I said, "Just a dream," and then I kissed him and he touched my face and we kissed again, and all that intensity turned into desire and I just wanted to be close to him, as close as possible. And either I was in the Safe Zone or I was pregnant, so right that second there was no need for birth control, and I didn't even know if we were fully awake, but our bodies knew what to do.

27

Then something a little spooky happened. The next morning when I woke up I knew I'd been dreaming again, though I didn't remember about what, and even before I opened my eyes I had these words in my mouth: *His name is Sasha.* And still half-asleep I thought, *Yes, that makes sense.* And then I thought, *Wait, who?*

The image of the baby from my dream the night before came rushing back, and I saw his big brown eyes and his round head, and I kept thinking, *Sasha...Sasha...* And then I just felt so naked and exposed I had a hard time getting out of the bed. George wasn't with me, he was at his house, and I had the urge to call him on the phone but I didn't want to go overboard. I grabbed my clothes and stuffed them under the covers and I got dressed under there like I used to on cold mornings when I was a kid.

I didn't see Renee downstairs, she was over at Dylan's, and while riding the bus to school I started thinking about all the kids I used to babysit, especially when I was thirteen and fourteen, since those were my peak babysitting years. One summer in Ukiah I had a job taking care of a baby girl named Estella. I had to do all the things you do with babies—change her diapers, feed her mushy foods with a spoon, put her down for naps, and keep her from eating the dirt out of the potted plants. Once I had her in a wading pool outside with her little floaty toys. She was old enough to pull herself to standing on the edge, but she slipped and fell and got so upset I had to carry her around while she cried.

Estella was cute and I liked her a lot, but taking care of her and the other kids I babysat still didn't amount to a whole lot of experience, nothing near what it would be like to be an actual parent. And now this imaginary baby named Sasha was filling up my mind. Or maybe he wasn't exactly imaginary, that was the problem.

* * *

That afternoon during a slow moment at work I found myself adding up the months on a piece of scrap paper. If I was really pregnant and had the baby it would be born around December, and I'd have about six months left of school until I graduated. I'd had a classmate once, an older woman who was pregnant at the beginning of the term. She disappeared for a week, and when she came back to class she brought the baby with her. She sat there taking notes with him sleeping in a carrier on her lap, or she put a blanket on the floor and he slept there, or if he was awake he just kind of goggled his eyes around the room.

I even went further with adding things up, thinking how if George and I lived together and shared a bedroom it would save a lot on rent. And I kept on calculating, as if the question could be solved with a bit of math, until suddenly I heard, "What are you writing so intently?"

I was standing at one of the counters, hunched over the paper, and I immediately crumpled it up into a ball. When I turned around, Calvin was looking at me strangely.

He said, "Is it a secret?"

I was sure my face was flaming red. I said, "It's nothing, just sketching out an idea," like I wasn't losing my mind.

He goes, "Oh, okay." And then, "Look what Tristan gave me." He pulled a little book from one of the zippered pockets on his leather jacket, *Chess for Beginners*, and handed it to me.

I laughed. "Are you reading this?"

"Hey!" He snatched it back. "It's interesting."

Calvin and Tristan had gotten a lot more serious in the past two years. They were even sharing an apartment downtown.

I said, "Is he teaching you to play?"

"Ever since I finally gave in." He put the book back in his pocket. "See what love does to you? Makes you consider things you thought you never would."

At that I pretty much turned to jelly. I even felt see-through. I whispered, "That's the truth."

* * *

Two days later there was still nothing. It was Saturday, cloudy but not raining, and George and I took a walk around Capitol Lake downtown. At one point we were standing by the water watching the ducks and this couple ambled by with a baby in a stroller. George gave me a look and put his arm around my shoulders. And then two more days passed and it was the twelfth day. I had a late afternoon dance practice and George picked me up again and when we got in the truck he looked at me and said, "No change, huh?"

I shook my head. "I'm just thinking a lot."

"Yeah." And we were pretty quiet on the drive to my house.

When we got there, we parked in front but we didn't get out. George held my hand and rubbed the back of it with his thumb.

I said, "What would you do? Like what would you do, if it was entirely up to you?"

He didn't want to say. He kept saying it had to be what I wanted, it was my body, and that he'd support me. But I said, "Please, just tell me. I want to know what you're feeling about it."

He looked out the front a long time, and he started to say something but stopped again, and then finally he goes, "Just me? What I'd want?"

My heart was beating hard. "Yeah."

"Well," he looked at me, "I might want to keep it."

That kind of floored me. I thought about my dream and what a good dad I was sure he'd be, and for a minute I was speechless. And then he goes, "But like I said--"

"I know, I know." I pressed my cheek to his shoulder.

* * *

I couldn't concentrate on anything the next day. I went to class and to work but I didn't feel like I was there at all. I kept thinking about this baby called Sasha and picturing Renee and Hafsa and Amy and Calvin and everyone telling me I'd gone off the deep end. They'd be angry and then they'd be distant. I could see my mom convinced I'd failed again, and all my friends going out while I stayed home, and them not wanting to hang out and feeling like we didn't have anything to talk about anymore, and I was just overwhelmed by all of it.

But then riding the bus home at the end of the day I realized that I'd only been seeing things from a certain perspective, as if this possible baby would happen to me alone and the whole responsibility and loneliness of it would crush me. Something switched then and I started looking at it from a different angle. I had a vision of George, laughing, with the baby in a backpack; Paulo as an uncle, running around with the kid at a park and falling down on purpose any time the kid fell down; and George's mom, Angela, with her sewing machine, making little blankets and overalls and telling us what to do when the kid got sick. Even my parents, with the distance and everything, would play a role. I didn't know how, but maybe it wouldn't just be eye-rolling disapproval, like I'd imagined at first. It might be other than that, something better, and I saw myself, maybe for the first time, within the web of a real family.

* * *

By the next day there was still no change. In one more day I'd go get a test, but I was already pretty convinced there was a seed of a baby growing in there. I had two morning classes and then a long break before my shift at work and I decided to take a walk to the farm.

I walked the path through the forest and all around the farm where everything was green and coming to life. I breathed in and out with every step and just worked on getting quiet. I was looking for the truth, my own truth, and while I was walking all those pictures I'd been seeing fell one by one, the images and the doubts and all the worried thoughts dissolved and all that was left was the grass under my feet, and the ground under that, and the clear air all around me, and then the answer was clear too.

I realized that this was something I wanted to do with George. It knocked my heart over, and tears came up. I wanted this with George and I wanted it for myself.

But not yet.

I imagined that seed in there, a little seed made by George and me, and I said I was sorry, but it was too soon. I'd get a test and if it was really for sure I'd go to the clinic. It was a relief to know, but the funny thing about it was the sudden sadness I felt. If there was going to be a little boy named Sasha, I hoped I'd meet him one day.

* * *

When I got to George's house that evening he was just out of the shower and Paulo was cooking. I figured George had said something to him because Paulo didn't want any help in the kitchen. He said, "You guys hang out, I've got it."

We sat on George's bed and he touched my hair and asked me how I was doing, and I said, "I can't have a baby now."

He nodded and took my hand. "Okay. Good."

My voice started shaking and I said, "I'm not ready yet."

And he goes, "Yeah, I get it. I'm with you. I mean, I love you. Jesus." He grabbed me in a big hug.

"But can I take a rain check?" I said it into his neck.

"A what?"

"A rain check. For down the road."

He moved back a bit and looked at me a long time and then he said, "Of course you can. I would love that." He shivered like he'd gotten a chill and stuck out his forearms. "Goosebumps."

* * *

That night I dreamed that Renee was throwing boomerangs and they kept hitting me in the gut, and when I woke up in the morning and went to the bathroom there was blood on my underwear. I was so shocked and relieved I almost passed out, and when I told George I started crying. He held me and said he was really glad. Really, really glad, because I wouldn't have to go through everything we thought, and then we just lay there, until it was time to get up and start the day.

* * *

I'd never been so happy to see blood in my life. I had cramps all day, but unlike my usual annoyance I was so thankful for them it was like I'd won the lottery. I wondered what the hell had happened, because over the next few days my period proceeded as it usually did. *The Natural Woman* said that sometimes women could be pregnant and not know it because they'd have an early miscarriage, and that might be marked by extra flow and clotting, but I didn't even see any of that. And after being so worried and convinced about being pregnant, now I thought maybe it was just a fluke and nothing at all. Whichever way, though, I decided to do more research and figure out ways to do the birth control thing with more emphasis on the control part.

Back at home, I found Renee in the living room and told her in a low voice, because Tom was in the kitchen, and she goes, "Halleluyah!" And then she shouted up to Hafsa that I was in the clear.

I said "Don't yell for fucksake!" I was blushing like mad, but Hafsa came charging down the stairs and they started doing a little tango, and I just turned into a laughing puddle on the couch.

Toward the end of May, the dance class got busy with the final performances. We all chipped in for a gift for Dr. Sundara, a colorful little tapestry with an elephant on it and mirrors around the edges because she'd told us once that she was in love with elephants. And then it was June and everything final was due and George and Paulo were super busy with their boating business, and Anita asked me if I wanted to help make decorations for the wedding. Of course I did because I always wanted to hang out with Anita, and I started going to her house in the evenings to make paper flowers and lanterns with her and Racine. And finally, in July, when the big day came, George and I got dressed up and we went.

* * *

We got to the place early and had time to walk around. It was on a farm that belonged to friends of theirs, with a big old empty barn that was all decorated and a grassy area around it with fruit trees, and way down at the end of a long driveway there was a stretch of forest and a little beach on the inlet. Anita's sisters and aunts were busy directing everything and they shooed us away, so George and I walked down to the water. It was a sunny day with a warm breeze and we walked on the last part of the gravel road holding hands.

George had on the only dress shirt I'd ever seen him in, rust-colored linen, and a pair of nice tan pants, with the poem he was going to read folded up in his pocket, and I was wearing a sleeveless dress that George's mom actually made for me. At the end of June when we were visiting she pulled out this big piece of blue fabric with miniature green polka dots and asked me if I liked it. When I said yes, she said she thought it would make a cute summer dress and she showed me a few patterns.

I hadn't been to many weddings and I asked George if he had. He said a handful, but that this was the first one with a couple that he was so close to.

I said, "Are you nervous about reading the poem?"

"Maybe a bit."

Down at the beach there was a shady area and driftwood here and there and a mix of sand and pebbles in between the bigger rocks. I wanted to wade in the water but George just wanted to sit a while. Paulo was working half the day and would be out later, but he made George take the whole day off. So, while George sat I kicked off my shoes and stepped into the water. The little waves lapped at my knees and the smooth rocks rolled under my feet.

George was leaning on a driftwood log. A breeze ruffled his hair in the front and made one point of his collar stick up, and after a while I asked him what he was thinking.

He said, "Not much. Nothing in particular." He smiled a little. "Just maybe about love. But it's more of a feeling."

I said, "It's a special day."

"It is."

And then he said, "Can you come over here?"

I sat down next to him and he put his arms around me. He said, "I just want to feel you."

* * *

The ceremony was very musical, with three of their friends playing--flute, guitar and cello. Marco looked great in his navy-blue suit that made his arms and legs look like stovepipes, and his flowered shirt and shaggy head on top like a lion. Anita was in the dress she'd made from two silk kimonos and if anyone looked like a goddess it was her, with flowers woven into her long black hair and the dress all the way to the ground.

When it was his turn, George got up to read the poem, one by Rumi. He read,

> *This is love: to fly toward a secret sky,*
> *to cause a hundred veils to fall each moment...*

He read another few lines and his voice choked up and he paused a second and then finished. When he sat down again I took his hand and kissed it and held it in my lap.

And then they were married, and the sun was on its way down and everyone was eating and making toasts. Then the dancing started, the barn glowing in all kinds of colors from the lanterns we'd made, and when we danced George held me so close. I felt like I'd never been more in love with him and I whispered, "I love you," in his ear and I don't think he heard it over the music, but I think he knew anyway.

*　*　*

Finally, when we stumbled in the dark down the driveway to the truck most of the other cars had already cleared out. The day had been beautiful and the night was beautiful too, but it was getting cold. I had my sweater on but my legs were bare and my teeth started chattering, and George said he'd get one of the blankets out of the back for the ride. But when he opened the hatch I scrambled in and I covered myself up, and I couldn't help it, I just started giggling like a madwoman.

George goes, "What are you doing?"

And I said, "Just come find me."

He climbed in too and I pulled him on top of me, and as we kissed he pushed my dress up over my hips and he tugged at my underwear. "Can I take these off?"

"Yeah." I was breathless. He pulled them off and kissed my legs, and I reached for his belt and got his pants down far enough.

And in between kisses he whispered, "Do we need protection?" and I said no, because I knew I was well into the Safe Zone. And he said, "Positive?"

I whispered back, "Positive."

I put my hands on his stomach and moved on top of him, and veil after veil fell, until it was all cymbals reverberating and the two of us tied up together in a sailor's knot. And before long we fell asleep, down into deep, dark currents of sleep that carried us, and in my dreams the stars turned overhead in an endless wheel.

I dreamed of the secret sky, like in the Rumi poem that George read, where the colors shifted, where they were soft or when they blazed, or when it was the vast pure blue of breathing. Or quiet drops of rain, touching the ground like fingertips.

And then there was another vision of the sky, a sky crossed with seven rainbows, one after the other, written out like a message on a tablet. It stretched over miles and miles of rain and sun and highway, telling me not to worry, because I was headed in the right direction.

The sky was overhead and it was even underfoot. It was everywhere.

And when I woke up, the hatch window was pale with light.

NOTES ON SEXUAL HEALTH

Since *Eighteen* takes place in the late 1980's to early 1990's, some of the facts related to sexual health that Talia deals with are different than today. While HIV is still a dangerous infection, for those who have access to treatment it is not usually the death sentence it was in years past. The technology around pregnancy tests has also become more sophisticated. Over-the-counter pregnancy tests used to be effective only after a pregnancy had advanced a minimum of four weeks, now it can take only a day or two after conception to test. Fertility observation is a viable method of birth control, for those who are well informed and practiced, but no method of birth control is 100% effective. Further, fertility observation offers no protection from sexually transmitted infections, such as HIV and other infections that can cause serious health problems.

ACKNOWLEDGMENTS

Many thanks to Natasha LaRoche, Heather Jarry, Genvieve Weber, Erika Lunder, Chris O'Connor, Chris Wolfe, Leah Catwrangleur, Meegan Simpson-Cooke, Skye Ladell, Jacki Taylor, Colleen Frary, and Suzanne Macdhomhail for early reading and helpful feedback. Special thanks to Patricia Kidd, Nadine Ijaz, Leora Hoshall, and Michelle Mulder for in-depth reading and insight, to the Room Six Water Ski Club for our kick-ass shop-talking meetings; to Chris and Asa for their ongoing love and support even when they don't agree with me, and to the team at Black Rose Writing for their hard work, dedication, and skill. Above all, eternal gratitude to Neesa Sonoquie, my greatest writing teacher and editorial Kung Fu master.

ABOUT THE AUTHOR

Jenny Jaeckel is the award-winning author and illustrator of several books including her historical fiction companion novels *House of Rougeaux* and *Boy, Falling*, a collection of illustrated short fiction entitled *For the Love of Meat*, and the graphic novel *memoir Spot 12: Five Months in the Neonatal ICU*. When not writing, Jaeckel works as an editor and translator. She lives in Victoria, British Columbia, with her family. *Eighteen* is her third novel.

NOTE FROM THE AUTHOR

Word-of-mouth is crucial for any author to succeed. If you enjoyed *Eighteen*, please leave a review online—anywhere you are able. Even if it's just a sentence or two. It would make all the difference and would be very much appreciated.

Thanks!
Jenny Jaeckel

We hope you enjoyed reading this title from:

BLACK ROSE
writing™

www.blackrosewriting.com

Subscribe to our mailing list – *The Rosevine* – and receive **FREE** books, daily deals, and stay current with news about upcoming releases and our hottest authors.
Scan the QR code below to sign up.

Already a subscriber? Please accept a sincere thank you for being a fan of Black Rose Writing authors.

View other Black Rose Writing titles at www.blackrosewriting.com/books and use promo code **PRINT** to receive a **20% discount** when purchasing.